'It's up to yo[...]
grave; even a[...] Zigger.
We rely on yo[...] . . . But you won't fail,
you've never failed yet.'

Zigger said nothing. He merely returned the
steady gaze of the Captain's eyes. Blue-grey eyes
they were, blue-grey like the spacesuit he wore.
And bright as the visor of the space helmet the
Captain held in the crook of his arm. A good
man, a fine captain. But worried.

Zigger nodded, saluted and went to work.
Already his mind had completed the list of what
he would need to complete the task that lay
ahead.

First, the Thermic Bombs . . .

But Zigger's mission is not quite what it seems
in *Living Fire*, the first story in this collection of
exciting new tales from Nicholas Fisk, one of the
best-known writers of science fiction for young
readers.

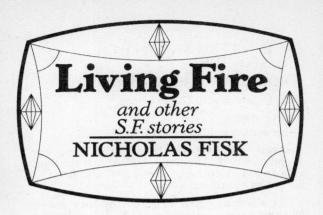

Living Fire
*and other
S.F. stories*

NICHOLAS FISK

Illustrated by
David Parkins

CORGI BOOKS

LIVING FIRE AND OTHER S.F. STORIES

A CORGI BOOK 0 552 524530

First publication in Great Britain

PRINTING HISTORY
Corgi edition published 1987

This book is set in 14/18 pt Century Schoolbook by Colset Private Limited, Singapore.

Corgi Books are published by Transworld Publishers Ltd., 61–63 Uxbridge Road, Ealing, London W5 5SA, in Australia by Transworld Publishers (Australia) Pty. Ltd., 15–23 Helles Avenue, Moorebank, NSW 2170, and in New Zealand by Transworld Publishers (N.Z.) Ltd., Cnr. Moselle and Waipareira Avenues, Henderson, Auckland.

Made and printed in Great Britain by Cox & Wyman Ltd., Reading, Berks.

Living Fire

and other
S.F. stories

Contents

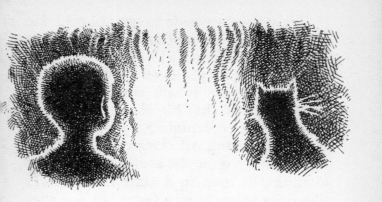

Living Fire

Zigger's granny said, 'Suppose I must get the washing in before it gets dark, oh dear me, and the lunch things still in the sink, I don't know. And it's turning so chilly you'd think it was winter. A nice fire, that's what we'll have, a real blizzy. You get the fire going, Zigger, there's a good boy, there's nothing like a fire. You'll need to get some coal in — what's that dratted cat doing on the table? Shoo, shoo! After the butter, the old devil, I know his ways. Yes, you get the coal, we'll need more coal, and then we'll have a blaze, a real blizzy . . .'

Zigger went outside to get the coal. He thought, 'It's not all that cold, but I suppose she feels it more . . . Well, she's old. Seventy. Seventy! Seven times as old as me. And old-fashioned. Washing on the line, coal fires, that big old cat.'

He was not complaining; just thinking. He liked staying with Gran. He liked seeing washing on a clothes line instead of looping the loop in a tumble drier. He liked the special voice Gran put on, ever so ladylike, when she answered the phone. And he liked the coal fire.

'A living fire' she called it. And she was right.

He took the washing off the line for her, then filled the coal box. She came out, saw the washing in the wicker basket, said, 'Oh! Aren't you a thoughtful boy!' and took it in. Zigger lugged the coal box through the kitchen, said, 'Gerroff!' to Satan, the black cat, who was on the table again, eyeing the butter, and put the coal box at the side of the fireplace. He knelt in front of the fire, staring at it.

Dead. Dust and ashes. 'Well,' he said to himself, 'we'll soon fix that! Soon you'll be alive again, with little tongues of flame darting about and smoke curling round itself and rushing up the chimney. Later, you'll be a fine old lazy, red and gold monster, crinkling and crackling, flaring and flaming; with burning caves and fiery pictures inside you . . .'

Gran came in and saw him kneeling there, staring. 'Dreaming again!' she said. 'You're awful, yes you are, oh dear me!' She was smiling, of course. 'You get that fire going, there's a love, and I'll see to the dishes, where's the dishcloth gone, oh there it is. Yes, you see to the fire, that's up to you.'

'It's up to you,' the Captain said. His voice was grave; even a little afraid. 'All up to you, Zigger. We rely on you. If you fail . . . But you won't fail, you've never failed yet.'

Zigger said nothing. He merely returned the steady gaze of the Captain's eyes. Blue-grey eyes they were, blue-grey like the spacesuit he wore. And bright as the visor of the space helmet the Captain held in the crook of his arm. A good man, a fine captain. But worried.

Zigger nodded, saluted and went to work. Already his mind had completed the list of what he would need to complete the task that lay ahead.

First, the Thermic Bombs.

He opened the Top Security locker with his Priority codecard and removed a packet. REDDIFLAME, the packet said. There was even a crude picture of a fire, topped with brightly coloured flames. Zigger smiled sardonically. A security measure, of course. Clever camouflage. Zigger knew — who better? — what the packet really contained. Thermic bombs!

With sure, steady fingers he opened the flap of the packet and (careful, now, very careful!) slid out the bombs. They were in a block. Each bomb had to be broken away individually. Faint lines showed the breaking points.

'Right!' he murmured. 'Here . . . we . . . go!' He applied pressure. He knew exactly how much to use. Too little — or too much for that matter — and you'd get an uneven break. An irregular fission of this sort could, it was rumoured, start a chain explosion, an uncontrolled holo-caust that would range through the whole Galaxy.

With an almost inaudible *snap*, a thermic bomb separated. Perfect. A tidy, unbroken oblong. Zigger let go the breath he had been holding and thought, 'OK. Stage One completed, but only Stage One. Now to construct the Energy Pile. Get on with it, man!'

He got on with it. Almost casually — for the risky part was over for the moment — he tossed the thermic bomb on top of the Launching Pad. The bomb lay there, white and innocent, very brilliant against the dull lattice of special metals that formed the pad. White, harmless, almost friendly . . .

How different from what came next — the glittering black Solar Capsules! These had the power of the sun itself locked within them. They had to be handled with kid gloves.

Kid gloves . . . Yet all Mission Control had supplied was this single Hand Protector! Zigger picked it up and stared disgustedly at it. An obsolete pattern; and damaged at that. He let the thing drop and settled back on his heels to think. Ah, of course. He'd have to rely on the Remote Handler: a clumsy apparatus, tricky to use even in expert hands. But Zigger was no ordinary expert.

He flexed the handler and said, 'OK. Operational.' With the skill born of long experience, he used the muscular movements of his own right hand to manipulate the jaws at the end of the remote handler. 'Come on, now . . .' he said to the handler. 'Come on, come on . . . gently does it . . .' The jaws closed, very slowly but very certainly. *'Lift!'* Zigger grated — and began lifting. It was easy when you knew how. Zigger knew how.

Again and again he repeated the actions — select, close jaws, lock on, lift, transport, position, disengage. Soon a heaped pile of solar capsules almost hid the thermic bomb. Almost, but not quite. There had to be a place left open, of course. A flame path, an ignition trail, a gap to admit the Igniter. 'Steady now,' Zigger whispered. He was actually using his naked fingertip to clear exactly the right space.

The Alien must have heard Zigger's whispered words — for it was there, beside him! It had moved on silent feet, with incredible stealth, seeking out human company.

Zigger made no move, showed no surprise. He was used to alien beings. Some flew, some scuttled, some crawled. Some even lived underground. So? So you came

14

to terms with them. You played it cool.

This Alien was of a species that walked silently — probed fearlessly — and invaded, remorselessly, the habitats of mankind. It pushed its face closer and closer towards Zigger's. Its blank, unyielding eyes, metallic gold, stared unblinkingly into his. Zigger did not refuse the challenge. 'Well, what do you want?' he demanded, his voice hard and clear. As he spoke, he knew how meaningless his words were. Few Aliens had mastered even the simplest human speech: this species seemed deliberately to ignore it.

The Alien made its move! Its blunt, black head, driven by the full power of the splendidly muscled body, hit Zigger square on the forehead. There was no pain — just this sudden, jolting, totally unexpected impact.

Zigger rocked on his heels — recovered his balance — grated, 'You devil!' and gave back blow for blow, forehead to forehead.

The Alien knew its master. It retreated. It sat and stared, at first in silence. But then it began to make its low, rumbling sound . . .

'Where's that dratted cat?' Gran called from the kitchen.

'He's all right, Gran. He's here, with me.'

'What's he up to?'

'He's purring.'

'Well, as long as he's not at the food, *that's* all right. How are you getting on?'

'How are you getting on?' the Captain said. He was trying to sound at ease and unworried.

Zigger merely pointed a finger in reply. The Captain took in what had already been accomplished and slowly nodded his head. 'I knew I could rely on you,' he said. 'And, Zigger, as you know better than anyone, maintenance of correct temperatures is vital to the success of this operation —'

'I'll see it through, sir. Rely on me.'

'I do, I do! And when the job's done, you won't be forgotten, Zigger. Rely on me for that!' The Captain's mouth worked briefly with strong emotion; then he nodded and was gone.

Somewhere in the distance, bells shrilled. There was a definite pattern to the ringing. The Alien heard. It turned its head to the source of the sound; then looked at Zigger, a question in its eyes.

'Even if I explained,' Zigger said, 'you wouldn't understand.' The bells continued their wild clamour; then suddenly ceased. 'Perhaps,' Zigger said, 'it's better that you *don't* understand. So many complications and contradictions . . .' The Alien stared at him with large, uncomprehending eyes. Zigger shrugged. 'All that matters to you, old chap,' he said, 'is that I complete my mission.'

He clenched his jaws and returned to his task. He checked and double-checked. Thermic bomb? Positioned and ready to go. Solar capsules? Fine — an ideal ignition pattern. That left the igniters — the triggers, the means of initiating the whole operation. *Where were they? Where were the igniters?*

For a brief instant, Zigger's heart stopped.

It was the Alien who resolved the crisis. It rose to its feet, arched the massive ridges of muscle along its spine, waved its fifth limb — and there they were! The igniters! The black bulk of the Alien had concealed them.

Gasping with relief, Zigger flung himself on the vital little container. 'Imbecile!' he hissed at the Alien. 'Don't you see — without these, we would have remained for ever in Status Standby! We would hold and hold, with the temperature constantly falling! — with conditions becoming, hour by hour, minute by minute, ever more intolerable!'

He checked himself. 'What's the use of blaming *you*?' he said, in a low voice. 'You simply don't understand ...' The Alien blinked and stared. Zigger braced himself and got back to work.

Using the forefinger of his right hand as if it were the piston of some precision machine, he slid open the inner section of the container. He extracted a single igniter and stared at it, wondering if one would be enough. Often he had succeeded with just one igniter, but there was always the lingering doubt ... 'Oh, get on!' he told himself. 'You're deliberately wasting time!' Time mustn't be wasted. The thing had to be done and now was the time to do it.

In the distance the bells rang once. 'Did-dang!' they said, and were silent. Zigger knew full well what the sound of the bells meant: the end. Time had run out.

He raised his head, straightened his shoulders and took a deep breath. Then, holding the small container in his left hand and the igniter in his right, *he struck*.

He struck — and a spark spurted, twinkled, glowed, died. He struck again and, cursing, yet again.

At last a flame flickered, dwindled, but

then grew triumphantly! It leapt outwards, always growing! Narrow-eyed, Zigger stared at the flame, willing it to grow stronger, knowing that when it did he would not have to strike again.

The flame steadied. The climactic moment had come!

Almost as if completing a sacrament, Zigger arched his body forwards, stretched out his rigid hand, and directed the flame, millimetre by millimetre, towards the flame path.

'Count down!' he muttered. 'Ten, nine, eight, seven, six, five . . .'

Gran came in. 'That was your Mum on the telephone,' she said. 'From a call box. They don't give you much time to talk, do they? You're hardly started before you're finished, oh dear me. Anyhow, they're in the car on their way back home and they're going to pick us up here and take us out to dinner in a restaurant, isn't that grand? An evening out for you and me both! So you needn't light the fire after all.'

So Zigger didn't.

Whooo-ooo Flupper!

This world is called Positos VI PH.
Wow, how I used to hate it!

'We're *prisoners*!' I'd shout. 'Never
allowed out of this crummy unit!'

'And if we *did* get out, what would we
do?' squeaked Lollo, my sister. She even
waved her fists, which was pretty useless
as she's only nine and small for her age.
I'm nearly twelve.

We stared out of the unit's window.
What did we see? A sort of grey-green
blancmange, with some dirty yellow
prehistoric-looking trees sticking out.
And that's all. 'I hate you,' muttered
Lollo.

I said nothing. What was there to say about Positos VI PH? The name tells you everything. The 'VI' means it's a sixth-order world — the smallest sort, the dregs. The 'PH' means 'partly hostile'. In other words, it has a tendency to kill humans. Charming.

'Let's play with the video,' I said.

'I'm sick of the video.'

'Chess, then.'

'You'll only win.' She chewed her lower lip for some time, then said, 'I'm going out.'

'You're not! It's not allowed!'

'I'm going *out*,' she repeated. I tried to stop her but she kept on putting on more and more outside gear. Even her helmet, although Positos air is breathable. Thick and muggy and smelly, but breathable.

I found myself doing what she was doing — donning boots, suit, bleeper and three sorts of weapon. It's no good arguing with Lollo. Anyhow, I'm supposed to take care of her. Big brother.

'We're off,' she said. Off we went. We followed the tracks of our parents' Ruff-stuff at first — the wide, deep tracks of its go-anywhere wheels. Mum and Dad are prospectors. They keep searching for something — anything — to sell back home, on Earth . It's a hard way to make a living.

The Ruffstuff's tracks swept off to the right so we kept walking to the left. We didn't want to meet them. We'd get told off. After a time, I said, 'Look, Lollo, that's enough. Let's go home.' But she just marched on.

We came to the swamp.

Today, it's known as Lolly's Lagoon because she saw it first. 'Lagoon' is a bit grand: it's really just a big old swamp, surrounded by droopy trees with their roots half in and half out of the water. And big mossy, fungus-like growths here and there on the shores. We stood and looked at it. Lollo made a face. I broke off a piece of wood or whatever it is from a tree, if that's a tree, and flung it at one of the huge pancake things like giant water-lily leaves that floated on the surface of the water. There was a damp *plaff!* as the soggy wood hit the soggy pancake. 'Good shot!' I was about to say —

When it moved! It rose! It reared up! It sort of humped up in the middle, sucking water with it, shrugging sprays of water from its wavy edges! It was alive!

23

It took off! Its fringe, its edges, became folded-over hydroplanes. The humped-up middle part was clear of the water. It made an upside-down U shape. Its fringes rippled and it moved. I mean, really *moved*. I fell over backwards in the slimy mud.

At first it just zoomed along, hydroplaning. But it had another trick up its sleeves. Suddenly the water inside the hollow of the U seemed to *boil*. Somewhere inside itself, the thing had a sort of jet propulsion.

Now it didn't just move. It accelerated like one of those old twentieth century water-speed-record breakers and *hurtled* over the water! It swept round in a huge curve. Lollo's mouth hung open. I gaped. It went so fast, we couldn't believe it. Then *hiss!* — *surge!* — *vroom!* — it headed straight for us like a thousand-mile-an-hour nightmare!

Now we were both on our backsides in the mud. But just as we thought it was going to flatten us, it somehow back-pedalled, slowed, cut its jets, rippled its fringes and turned pink. We stared at it and it seemed to stare at us.

Silence. Then the thing said, 'Whooo.'

Lollo whooed right back at it. I added a shaky whoo of my own.

The thing — it must have been five metres across — rippled its flanges invitingly and eased right to where we stood. It said, 'Whooo?'

You can guess what happened next. Lollo climbed aboard the thing. Her big brave brother followed. The thing said, 'Whooo!' and moved.

When we lived Earthside, Lollo and I tried everything: zeta-powered bikes, dune zoomers, no-grav gymnastics, the lot.

You can keep them all as long as you leave us Flupper.

Riding Flupper was Glory, Glory, Glory all the way. Not just the thrill of all that acceleration, all that speed, all that flying water. He was so *nice* about everything. He *wanted* us to be happy aboard him. He showed us the whole lagoon (it is very big), slowing down to let us see the most interesting parts, then hurtled off amid boiling clouds of spray to give us a thrill. He even realized that we might slide off him when he accelerated, and provided us with a vine, like a rope, to hang on to. He held on to the other end, it went underneath him.

Mum and Dad didn't find out about Flupper and us for more than a week. We faked the unit's video to show us 'in'. That was our only fear — being found out, being told 'No! Never again!' Meanwhile, Flupper showed us the deadly thorn bushes that wrap round their prey like octopuses: and then whooshed us off at savage speeds — sometimes so fast he aquaplaned over the water.

There were other Flupper-type lily pads, of course. They seemed to welcome us too. We called one the Clown because he used to follow Flupper, cutting him up and teasing him. All in fun, naturally. Flupper would pretend to skid and go out of control, it was terrific — we'd hang on like grim death to the rope.

We knew we were perfectly safe, of course. But we were wrong.

That day, we were on Flupper doing about a million miles an hour. The Clown was racing alongside and Lollo and I were showing off to him, whooing and waving. Lollo raised one leg and waggled her foot cheekily. Her other foot slipped.

She fell down. The rushing water

clutched at one of her legs. The pull of the water tore her off Flupper. For a second I glimpsed her wet, frightened face: then she was hurtling away from me, bouncing over the water like a rag doll, her arms and legs flailing.

She hit the blancmange of the shoreline, bounced over it and flew sprawling into some bushes. Poison thorn bushes.

She screamed. Loudly at first, then in an awful breathless sobbing way.

Flupper took me to the shore and I ran to Lollo. When I reached her, I stopped dead, appalled by what I saw. She was *red*, red all over. The thorns were cutting her to pieces. The bush wrapped itself tighter and tighter around her and the thorns kept going in.

Then the snake thing came. I had seen the snake things from a distance. This one had a prong like a dagger in its head. I was screaming at Flupper and dancing about in an agony of uselessness. I thought the snake thing wanted Lollo. It didn't. It dug its dagger into the roots of the bush. The bush was of a dirty purplish colour. As the dagger went in, the bush turned grey and all its thorns went pale and soft. It died almost instantly. Now the snake thing could go for Lollo.

But it was too slow, or too stupid: I just had time to grab her ankles and pull her away. I towed her over to the muddy shore and flung her aboard Flupper. I was yelling for Flupper to help, to do something, anything. But all he did was to leave the shore and head fast for another part of the lagoon, where the moulds and fungi overhang the water. I begged him not to, but he just went on, heading straight for them.

'Home, take me home!' I shouted to Flupper. He took no notice. I could say nothing to Lollo, she had become a silent, horrible, raw red thing. 'Not this way!' I shouted. 'Home!'

But still Flupper continued in the wrong direction, heading for the greyish clumps of mould and fungi. I hated those growths, they frightened me. And Flupper was not merely heading for them, he was in among them! 'No!' I screamed. But it was too late: the sticky greyish growths were brushing over Lollo's body, clinging to her, damply caressing her, sticking to her in wisps and clusters.

And Flupper had done this deliberately! I lay down on him and beat at him with my fists. I must have been out of my mind . . .

Suddenly it didn't matter any more. I lay there, head buried in my arms, knowing that Lollo was dead: I would spend the rest of my life cursing myself and Flupper. Cursing and weeping.

Then Lollo's voice said, close to my ear, 'Yuck! I am filthy! All *bloody*!'

I sat up and she was kneeling beside me, picking at herself disgustedly, trying to

29

get rid of the fungi and moulds. And —
unbelievably — *as I watched, the cuts and
stabs in her flesh healed.*

'All this *blood*,' she said, in just the
same voice she'd have used if she'd
spotted chocolate round my mouth. 'How
disgusting! You'll have to get it off. I
can't.'

Later, I helped her sponge off the caked
blood. It took a long time, there was so
much of it. We did it at home back at the
unit. We never got rid of the stains on her
gear. Those stains gave us away, of
course. Dad spotted them and Mum tore
us apart. A real tongue-lashing. Almost
as bad as the thorn bush, Lollo said.

Our parents wouldn't believe a word we
said, so we took them to see Flupper. Dad
carried a Trans Vox so that we could talk
properly with him. I'm amazed that Lollo
and I never thought of using the Trans
Vox: it translates almost any language
into our language. Soon, everyone was
talking away like mad.

A little later — just a few months — we
were rich. Rich as you can get!

All thanks to Flupper, of course. And
those growths that used to frighten me,

the moulds and fungi.

You know about penicillin? Alexander Fleming discovered it quite early in the twentieth century. The wonder antibiotic, the great cure-all. Well, *our* moulds and fungi (I mean, Flupper's) turned out to be super pencillin, penicillin $\times$ 10,000. And Dad and Mum had staked the claim so they have Galactic Rights.

So we were and are everlastingly rich. 'Just think!' Mum said. 'We can go back to our proper home! Live Earthside!'

'I don't want to go back home!' Lollo said. 'I *won't* go, you can't *make* me go!'

Flupper, of course: she couldn't bear the thought of leaving him. I felt the same.

When we talked to Flupper about it, he said, 'Do you know how old I am?' We said no. 'I'm 245 Earth years old,' he said. 'And I've got another 150 to go . . .'

So perhaps Lollo and I won't make so much fuss about going back to Earth. We can always come back. And Flupper will always be there.

'Whooo-ooo, Flupper!'

Monster

I was creeping through the low bushes, silently, carefully, keeping close to the ground — when suddenly, the Monster was there!

The alien Monster! It towered above me, swaying on its two enormous legs! It was so tall that its head seemed to disappear in the brightness of the sky: so wide that its shadow darkened the ground where I stood!

I froze.

But then our eyes met. And when they met, I knew all I needed to know.

The Monster, huge as it was, was also

weaker than me. Although it was power-ful, I was more powerful. I could master this Monster.

Neither of us moved. The Monster stared down at me. I stared back, hearing the wise words of the teachers who trained us to travel in space. 'If you meet alien beings,' they said, 'never turn your back! Face them, eye to eye! Your eyes are your first weapons: the eyes of a superior race!'

So I held my ground and stared. The Monster blinked its eyes, shifted its feet.

It felt my power. I felt its weakness.

Then, still holding the Monster with my eyes, I let my mind wander back. I remem-bered the long journey through space and its terrible ending . . .

Our ship smashed down on the alien world. I alone lived.

And at once, our wrecked ship was found and captured. That was very bad, for I was kept prisoner in the ship. For how long? Perhaps for ever? I did not know. I never saw the alien world, or my captors. All I saw was the hatch — the door of our ship — being turned. It would turn and go on turning until it was open and light from outside came through.

This meant that the aliens were once again coming for me. Two great armoured arms and hands reached through the hatch. One hand searched for me. I tried to escape. But always, the searching hand found me — gripped me — held me.

The other hand held a tube with a needle. This hand reached towards me. The needle went in. I fell down and a blackness came.

Later I woke up in my prison. I felt sore and strange. Obviously they had examined me.

It happened many times. I thought it would go on for ever. But one day they failed to screw down the hatch properly. I escaped.

Now, I have walked in their alien world.

And now I face one of their alien beings: the Monster!

I keep staring, feeling my power grow. The Monster shuffles its feet, waves a huge pronged hand and makes its first sound.

'*Poo see,*' it says.

The sounds mean nothing to me — except that the Monster is nervous.

'*Poo see?*' it repeats. It stretches out its pronged hand towards me: then draws it back. It cannot face the glare of my eyes!

I study the Monster. Weak! That is the word for it! Weak, untidy, grubby, badly put together . . .

Yes, the Monster is grubby. I am clean.

Most of the Monster's skin is raw and naked. I am covered all over with beautiful, silky, colourful hairs.

The Monster balances uneasily on two great legs. I stand at ease on four elegantly tapered legs.

The Monster wears a stupid sort of armour — stupid because it does not cover the head, the arms or most of the legs. Besides, the armour is made of various kinds of soft stuff, easy to claw through. I need no armour, of course. But then, I am from a superior race . . .

Poor, clumsy Monster.

From the distance, another alien voice calls. Here are the sounds it makes . . .

'Tim-mee! Cummand wosh yor hands for suppa!'

The Monster says, *'Spose I berra go,'* and turns from me, uncertainly. It gives me a last look . . .

'Niiiss poo see!' it says. I feel it wants to be friends. I do not.

I walk away from the Monster very

slowly, my tail held high.

Very soon, I meet the true rulers of this alien world.

Like me, these superior beings are beautiful — and modestly covered with fur. Like me, they move silently and neatly on four legs.

They have splendid tails like mine. They say very little because, most of the time, their tails speak their thoughts. They are friendly, yet their sharp claws and teeth are always ready for hunting and war.

I join them. Because I know things and have seen things that mark me out as different, I become their leader.

Together, we rule the alien world.

During the day, when the poor, clumsy Monsters on two legs make their fuss and noise, we sleep or doze. If we happen to wake up, we command the Monsters to serve us. They are good servants. They bring us food and drink, let us in and out of their shelters. If we feel that our chins need tickling or our backs stroking, the Monsters are happy to do it.

Then comes the night . . . and the world is all ours!

We sing our beautiful love songs under the moon.

We explore the wild and hidden places.

We search out the little scurrying, living toys, obviously made for our pleasure, and hunt them down.

What times we have! And how lucky I am to be one of the masters of this excellent world!

It *is* luck, of course — I admit that.

Things could have turned out very differently if I did not look as I do — if I did not look like one of the creatures which the Monsters call *'Niiiss poo see!'*

The Golden Lump

It was so cold that February morning that all the puddles were frozen and the sky was a lead sheet above the icy rooftops. Dipi's hands had warm brown skin because she was an Indian girl. But now the fingers sticking out of her mittens were a dull, dusty, purplish colour. They ached when she folded the newspapers and magazines and thrust them through the letterboxes.

Most of the time, Dipi enjoyed doing her paper round. She also enjoyed helping in the newspaper-tobacconist shop her parents ran. She liked the lights shining on bars of chocolates, magazines, cigarettes, tobaccos. She liked being liked: many customers knew her by name and there was always someone to joke with.

But the paper round on this icy winter's day was no joke. Dipi did her round early, so as to get home and enjoy a long, warming proper breakfast before going to school. Now the time was 6.40. A few lights, not many, were coming on in some houses. The street was still sunk in its chilly sleep.

Except for No. 27.

In No. 27 there was a light upstairs, a light in the hallway window, and light — bright light — from the rooms in the basement. It was always the same, however early you were. Always, the lights were on and someone was moving about. Always, you could hear electric motors humming or the thin scream of metal being worked with a power tool, or the tap of a hammer.

Mr Fewgitt's house, No. 27.

She had never seen Mr Fewgitt but her parents had told her about him. He was very old. He paid his paper bills every Friday afternoon. He was polite. He was strange. He read strange magazines that no one else read — dull, dusty-looking journals without pictures.

Dipi was getting Mr Fewgitt's batch folded and ready for the letterbox when the front door opened, an amazing face appeared, and a high, clear, ancient voice said, 'My dear young lady, you must be half frozen.'

It was Mr Fewgitt himself. Dipi stared at him. His face was amazing because it was so finely wrinkled. The wrinkles made spiders' webs round his pale grey eyes; and lace round the edges of his mouth. His hair was amazing too. It was not merely white. It had the whiteness of the finest nylon threads. Dipi had never seen so old a person.

Mr Fewgitt said, 'I have just prepared tea. *Hot* tea. You must drink a cup with me. I insist.'

Dipi should have said, 'No!' She knew that young girls don't have anything to do with strange men. But then Mr Fewgitt smiled and his smile produced a whole new crop of hair-fine wrinkles. Besides, it was a nice smile. Besides, warm air gusted out to her from the open door. Besides, Dipi wanted to see what went on in the basement.

So she followed Mr Fewgitt downstairs

and found herself in a very small room like an office. There was an old desk, many files and papers, an ancient typewriter called Bar-Lock, two chairs and a fat brown teapot with wisps of steam coming out of its curly spout.

'Pray be seated,' Mr Fewgitt said.

Dipi sat down, wishing she could think of something to say — and wishing, too, that she could see beyond the door into the rest of the basement, where Mr Fewgitt did whatever he did. She sipped her tea and it burned her mouth. 'Uff!' she spluttered. 'Grrrff! Ouch! Pardon!' Then, because she felt a fool, she blurted out, 'Are you *very* old, Mr Fewgitt?' As soon as she had said this, she felt more of a fool than ever.

Mr Fewgitt didn't mind in the least. He said, 'I don't think you would believe me, dear young lady, if I told you how old I am.'

Dipi said, 'Oh,' and tried to concentrate on drinking tea without choking. There was a silence.

The silence was broken by small sounds from the next room — the main part of the basement. The sound was of the sort Dipi had half-expected to hear: a high-pitched moan, a lonely and heart-rending sound. Mr Fewgitt took no notice. He stirred his tea and sipped it. But then again the moaning sound came: and yet again!

'Mr Fewgitt,' Dipi said, her voice trembling, 'what is happening there? What have you got in there?'

Mr Fewgitt put his cup down very slowly, and said, 'I beg your pardon?'

He looked and sounded completely innocent, but Dipi was not to be put off. '*What is in there?*' she demanded, fixing his pale grey eyes with her big, bold, brown ones.

Again the piteous moaning sound came. 'Ah!' said Mr Fewgitt, apparently only now understanding Dipi. 'That sound! From in there! You wish to know what it is?'

Dipi nodded her head. She could not speak.

Mr Fewgitt leaned across the desk. He stared at Dipi and said, 'May I ask if you are . . . a *brave* young lady?' Again Dipi nodded her head. 'Not afraid,' Mr Fewgitt continued, 'of wild animals?'

He spoke softly; but Dipi's voice was a mere frightened whisper. 'I want to know,' she said.

43

But her mind told her that she already knew. There would be a great wooden bench with a bandage-wrapped human figure clamped to it, and writhing electric fire from strange crackling machines, and a mad hunchback grinning as he pulled at the switches to step up the current . . . or there would be cages, each containing a hideous mutant, half beast and half human. And these monsters would tug at the bars and gibber and slaver. And eventually one would get loose . . .

She had seen it all in films and on the video cassettes her parents hired out. But now it was going to become real and true. Yet she could not resist it.

'Prepare yourself,' saidMr Fewgitt. He towered over her. He beckoned to the door leading to the other room, the chamber of horrors. 'Wild beasts,' he muttered as his hand slowly turned the doorknob. 'Teeth . . . claws . . . those wild eyes . . .' he said, shaking his head. Now the door was opening. 'Be so kind,' he said over his shoulder, 'as to bring the milk jug.'

His voice was like the film voices — kind, silky, polite yet horribly threatening — only much worse. The milk jug! Why a milk jug? But better to obey. Dipi seized the milk jug with a hand that trembled so violently that drops of milk jumped and spilled. Then she followed him into the laboratory, where the wild beasts waited . . .

At first Dipi could see nothing. The light from a reflector spot dazzled her. But soon she could see it all: the stained benches, the writhing assemblies of glass tubes and flasks, the electric machines, the circular saw with its glittering, vicious little teeth . . .

She took all this in and gazed around her wildly, trying to find the beasts. 'Where are they?' she cried.

The quiet, dry, smooth voice of Mr Fewgitt answered her. His long, bony, horny-nailed finger stretched out to point. 'Over there!' he said. 'Look out! They are emerging!'

There were three puppies. Their names were Freeman, Hardy and Willis. Each puppy was more delightful than the last. Hardy, the one with the spots on his tummy, was the one that made the moaning noise. 'He requires milk,' Mr Fewgitt explained. Dipi poured milk into a saucer and Hardy attacked it, spilling most of it in his enthusiasm. 'Wild beast!'

Mr Fewgitt said, shaking his head. 'Untutored savage. I did warn you.'

Willis, the black puppy with the white bits here and there, was the most desperate character of the three. Mr Fewgitt said so. Willis was a shoelace-biter. He gave small, tangled, snarling noises and pounced on Mr Fewgitt's laces. He attacked with such vigour that, often, he collapsed on his back, having tied himself into a sort of knot 'You would, would you?' said Mr Fewgitt with awful sternness as he bent down and tickled the puppy. 'Take that! and *that*!' he said. Willis, delighted, pretended to give Mr Fewgitt ferocious bites. But his mind was set on the shoelaces. He very nearly got one undone.

'I love Freeman best,' Dipi said, holding him out in front of her. 'Oh, look at his little whiskers! Pure white! Look, he's trying to lick my face! Look, Mr Fewgitt, do look!'

When Freeman, Hardy and Willis finished drinking milk, biting each other's ears, tumbling over each other and running over the slippery floor with wild skiddings and scrabblings, they all three climbed into a cardboard box lined with

newspaper and fell asleep in a heap. 'For the moment we are safe,' Mr Fewgitt said. 'But only for the moment. Let us drink more tea.'

They drank tea. Dipi said, 'But how did you *get* them? Where is their mother?'

'I fear I will never have the pleasure of her acquaintance,' said Mr Fewgitt. 'Nothing is known of the mother. All that I can be certain of is this: when I placed my refuse sacks by the dustbins at the back of these premises, I discovered a cardboard box — the very box you have seen — with three puppies inside it. A note attached to the box bore the message NOT WANTED. The word NOT was spelled with two 't's.' He shrugged his shoulders. 'I took it upon myself,' he said, 'to act *in loco parentis*.'

47

'What does that mean?'

'It means that I am now the mother, father, uncle, aunt and every other relation to the three unfortunate mongrels.'

'*I* think they're lucky. Lucky to have you. I mean, I think you're brill and they're brill.'

Mr Fewgitt accepted the compliment with a nod of his head. 'This tea,' he said, 'is distinctly *un*brill. It is stale. Shall I make some fresh?'

'Oh!' Dipi said, jumping up. 'My paper round! I must go!' She started fastening her coat. 'Oh dear!' she said. Then, 'May I come back?'

'At any time, dear young lady,' said Mr Fewgitt.

'You could call me Dipi. It's short for Dipika. May I come back this evening?'

'I am always here. You are always welcome. My given name is Tempus. I hope you will so address me.'

She left and went on with her paper round.

Dipi visited Tempus Fewgitt whenever she could, which was often. Each time she found the puppies bigger, better and more delightful. 'You must be terrific at being a local parentis or whatever it is,' she said one day. 'No puddles, no messes. Well, hardly any.'

'The secret,' replied Mr Fewgitt, 'is iron discipline. As soon as you leave, out come the whip, the ball and chain, and indeed the whole apparatus of rigorous repression.'

'I bet,' Dipika said. 'Oo! Quick! — Willis wants to do his duty!'

Mr Fewgitt picked up Willis, held him at arm's length and said, 'You are going out there a raw, untrained puppy-dog. But you are coming back a *star*.' Sure enough, Willis performed neatly on the tray, then wagged his tail and looked modest. 'Iron discipline,' said Mr Fewgitt.

Freeman remained Dipi's favourite. He had a white muzzle, a brown body, white paws and — best of all — a habit of rolling from side to side on his back to welcome Dipi. As he rolled, he waved his front paws and smirked. Then he licked her and wriggled his hindquarters. The other puppies were wonderful but, to Dipi, Freeman was the best.

She was fascinated by the puppies; but also fascinated by Mr Fewgitt. 'What do you *do* here all day — and all night?' she asked him.

She watched him as he carefully considered his answer. His head went back; the tips of his fingers were brought together; the amazingly fine white hair floated as his head moved.

'Work,' he answered at last.

'Yes, work, of course, but what do you actually *do*?'

A long silence; then Mr Fewgitt said, 'My work is to do with having the time of my life.'

'That's not work!' Dipi said. 'That's pleasure!'

'You think so?' he said. 'You really think so? I find it quite exhausting.' As he said this, he looked unbelievably old and weary. But all the same, his words made no sense to Dipi. 'Would you be so good,' he said, 'as to heat the water in the kettle to make tea?'

She got nothing more out of him.

As she made tea, she thought about him. He was old, yes. But also, in many ways, not old. He knew all sorts of things that old people were not expected to know: modern things. Yet he spoke like an out-of-date encyclopaedia. And he said

things that puzzled her. The other day
Dipi had said, 'No, my parents don't mind
me coming here. They just turn a blind
eye to it.'

'Nelson,' Mr Fewgitt said. 'Admiral
Nelson's famous blind eye.' He closed his
eyes, tilted his head back and added,
'What a genius — and what a fool — that
man is!'

'*Is?*' Dipi said. 'You mean *was.*'

Mr Fewgitt — Dipi never could bring
herself to call him 'Tempus' — then made
one of his puzzling remarks. 'What is the
date?' he asked.

'Fourteenth of March,' Dipi said.

'No, the *date*, the *date*!' he said. It was
the first time he had spoken crossly to
Dipi. Even now the crossness seemed to
come more from exhaustion than anger.

She repeated the date, this time adding
the year. She did this sarcastically, as if to
say, 'You want the date? OK, here it is, *all*
of it.'

The sarcasm was wasted. Mr Fewgitt
closed his eyes, shook his head and said
another puzzling thing. 'Learn to keep
time!' he muttered, waving his hand in a
slow rhythm. 'Don't lose time, don't lose
place!'

He was obviously talking to himself. Dipi did not understand his words — then.

The only sinister thing in the basement workroom was the 'coffin'. It was a narrow box two metres long. Dipi could just imagine a horror-film body lying in it, arms folded, eyes closed. Then the eyes snap wide open!— the body rises!— the mouth grins evilly, showing pointed fangs! *Euch!*

In fact, the 'coffin' was not sinister at all. Indeed it was the private resting place of Dipi's favourite puppy, Freeman. There were blankets folded up to pad the bottom of the 'coffin': Freeman trod the blankets into a nest, then settled down to sleep. He spent hours a day in the box.

The brightest things in the workroom were a collection of glass flasks with coloured liquids in them; and the gold lump. Dipi liked the lump. It was about the size of a grapefruit. It weighed a ton. Its knobbly surface was of a dull, uninteresting gold — but every so often, Mr Fewgitt cut a slice off it with his electric circular saw. This freshly cut surface shone gloriously: rich, gleaming, gold!

'It's fool's gold, isn't it?' Dipi said. 'Iron pyrites. We learned about it at school. Wouldn't it be great if it were *real* gold? Then you'd be rich, wouldn't you?'

'Quite so,' said Mr Fewgitt.

'Would you like to be rich? I would. If I were rich I could have anything I wanted.'

'You really think so?' said Mr Fewgitt.

'Well, almost anything. I suppose if you got ill, or something . . .'

'Or old,' said Mr Fewgitt.

'Mr Fewgitt . . . you are terribly old, aren't you? Do you *mind* being old? You don't seem to. You seem to have things organized, if you know what I mean.'

'A time and a place for everything,' Mr Fewgitt said. The puppy called Willis scrambled up on his lap. He stroked its ears.

'My parents spent most of their life looking for the right *place*,' Dipi said. 'And we ended up here, in England. My poor parents had terrible times —'

'Until they found the right place,' Mr Fewgitt said, finishing Dipi's sentence for her.

'That's right,' Dipi said. 'I mean, it's not perfect here, but at least we're alive.'

'Being alive,' Mr Fewgitt said, 'has its

53

advantages. One appreciates them more as one grows older.'

He said this without bitterness. Dipi thought, 'Poor Mr Fewgitt! He's got to die, quite soon. And he knows it. How much time does he have left? Will he die in this place?'

As if he had caught her thoughts, Mr Fewgitt said, 'I am glad you and your parents have found the right place. Very glad. But for some people, time matters more than place.'

Dipi said nothing. To have spoken her thoughts out loud would have embarrassed her. She looked at Mr Fewgitt's long, thin hand as it stroked the puppy. The hand was so old, the puppy was so young.

Mr Fewgitt said, 'I really must find the time somehow.'

'The time for *what*, Mr Fewgitt?'

'Oh, nothing in particular,' said Mr Fewgitt. 'Just the *right* time, that is all. Like your parents' right place.'

'Oh,' said Dipi, not understanding.

That day, Mr Fewgitt had been old and tired. Next day, Dipi found him completely changed: not young — he could never seem young — but somehow recharged.

She found him on all fours, being a puppy. Freeman and Willis, jiggling with joy, charged and retreated in front of him, falling over each other. Hardy attacked from behind. He had a shoelace in his mouth. He tugged ferociously at it, rolling his eyes and making fierce gargling noises.

'Dear young lady!' Mr Fewgitt said, straining his fragile neck to look up at Dipi. 'You could not have come at a more convenient time! The wild beasts attack me with unparalleled ferocity! You shall rescue me!'

'The kettle's boiling its head off,' Dipi said, sternly. 'Didn't you notice?'

'I did indeed, I did indeed,' said Mr Fewgitt. 'But unhappily I am unable to rise — back, sir, back!— from my present position. If I may crave your assistance . . . ?'

He stretched out a hand. Dipi took it and helped him to rise. He seemed without weight, without joints. It took some time to get him to his feet. He kept saying, 'Bow-wow!' or, 'Ah, would you!' to the delighted puppies instead of concentrating on getting up.

'You are silly,' Dipi said. She managed to detach Hardy from the shoelace and kissed the warm dome of his head. But with Mr Fewgitt she was stern and motherly. 'You might have got stuck in that position for ever,' she said. *'Really!'*

'For ever?' Mr Fewgitt replied. 'Oh no, I don't think so. I have other plans.' His eyes were very bright.

'What do you mean?' Dipi said. She made tea. 'What other plans?'

'Plans involving a — ha! — change of position.'

She poured tea and said, 'You're up to something.' She looked around for clues.

She saw the 'coffin'. It had been moved on its bench to bring it nearer a pile of apparatus perched on a trolley. The apparatus was made of laboratory flasks, curling glass piping and bits of plastic tube. It was all very complicated and unsafe-looking, but the glass items were polished clean.

'Go on, tell me about it ,' she said, fixing him with her intense brown eyes. For a moment she wondered if he had been drinking; but of course that was impossible. 'What are you all excited about?'

she demanded.

'I have been considering,' he said, 'taking an away break. That is the term, is it not?'

Dipi nodded. 'An away break,' she said. 'Fine. Where are you off to? Is it a nice place?'

Mr Fewgitt seemed puzzled by the question. Then, 'Oh, very nice.' There was still a secret light in his ancient eyes. Dipi mistrusted it.

'Is it far away?'

'Not near,' said Mr Fewgitt. 'But not too remote, either.'

'If you're going away,' Dipi insisted, 'why bother putting all this stuff together?' She nodded her head at the apparatus on the trolley. 'You can't take it *with* you, whatever it is,' she said.

'Quite so,' said Mr Fewgitt. 'But then, you see, there would be some difficulty in making the journey *without* it.' He seemed very pleased with this answer. He smiled. Dipi was not at all pleased.

'Look, Mr Fewgitt,' she said. 'Are you sure you will be all right? I mean, you're not very strong. And then there's money. If you got ill, or something, you'd need *money*.'

'Dear child, I never concern myself about money,' said Mr Fewgitt.

'Everyone else has to,' Dipi said.

'They do indeed, they do indeed,' said Mr Fewgitt. 'The tea you so kindly prepared will soon be undrinkable,' he said. Then he did something that never failed to amuse yet please Dipi: he offered her his arm. She took it, feeling she ought to curtsey and flutter a fan.

Arm in arm, they entered the little office. The puppies, exhausted, scratched, yawned and fell asleep. Dipi and Mr Fewgitt drank their tea undisturbed, he on one side of the desk and she on the other. It was all very formal and restful.

The arm-in-arm business was not uncommon. But when Dipi prepared to leave, Mr Fewgitt did something he had never done before. In his pale, cold fingers, he took Dipi's warm, brown hand, raised it to his lips, and kissed it. His lips felt like tissue paper against her skin.

'My dear young lady,' he said, 'you have no idea how I shall — ' He stopped.

Dipi said, 'Yes, Mr Fewgitt? How you shall *what*?'

'How I shall enjoy a second cup of tea on this chilly morning,' said Mr Fewgitt.

The door closed slowly on his amazingly wrinkled smile. Dipi, in the street, looked back and caught a last glimpse of him.

She never saw him again.

Because her paper round started so early, Dipi was among the first to arrive on the scene. The firemen were packing up to leave, but the police were still there. A few neighbours stood about in their night-clothes, gawping.

'Ah, Miss,' said the Police Sergeant. 'Just the one I've been waiting for. They tell me you know Mr Fewgitt better than anyone. Perhaps you can assist in our enquiries?'

The windows of the basement were blown out. Steamy smoke still curled upwards, but the firemen had seen to whatever real fire there had been. 'An explosion,' the Sergeant explained. 'About an hour and a half ago. Nothing very serious.'

'Where's Mr Fewgitt?' Dipi said in a hoarse whisper.

'Where indeed. That's why I want to talk to you,' said the Sergeant.

'But he must be in there, he's always there!' Dipi cried. She threw her bike down on the pavement and ran to the basement.

The Sergeant did not try to stop her. He simply followed her. 'You won't find him, Miss,' he said. 'Definitely not. He's gone. Not a trace of him.'

'The puppies! Where are the puppies?'

Now the Sergeant was interested. 'Puppies, Miss? What puppies? Suppose you sit down in that chair and tell me what goes on in these premises? Sit down, Miss, do.'

But Dipi was already through the door leading from the little office to the basement workroom; and her wide eyes were taking in everything.

She saw at a glance what had happened. The tower of apparatus on the trolley had exploded, or tumbled, or something of the sort. And from that moment on —

'That's right, Miss,' said the Sergeant, following her eyes. 'That's what started it.'

She did not answer. She went to the 'coffin'. She saw what she expected. Instead of the rumpled, circular patch that Freeman trod for himself each night, the blankets showed the clear imprint of a body. The head here, the feet there. She wondered how long it had taken Mr Fewgitt to clamber in. He had used this chair as a ladder and he must have held on to this corner of the bench . . .

She could almost see him doing it. She could also see, for the first time, a dozen other things: all of them incredible, unbelievable, yet obvious.

'You said "Puppies", Miss,' said the Sergeant.

Dipi thought. *'He's* gone. Gone on his away break. He couldn't have left the puppies behind to starve, he'd never do that, he's not cruel.'

But then she heard a whimpering noise.

She traced the noise through the litter of broken glass, overturned cardboard cartons and scattered papers to a dark corner crowded with dusty files and boxes. 'Come out,' she said. 'It's safe! Be good, it's me, Dipi! Come out!'

Freeman came out, his little tail down, his round eyes bleary with fright. He whimpered at Dipi and began to wag his tail. But he also wriggled with embarrassment and looked behind him. He had made a mess. 'That's all right, Freeman, really it is!' Dipi said. She picked him up and cuddled him. At once he cheered up and licked her face as hard as he could.

'You said *"puppies"*, Miss,' the Sergeant repeated. 'How many puppies?'

Dipi thought before answering. 'He'd not take them all,' she thought. 'He'd leave me my favourite, my darling Freeman. I'd better look, but I'm sure there'll only be Freeman.'

To the Sergeant she said, 'Just the one puppy. I remember now. There were three but he — he found a new home for the others.'

Freeman stopped licking her. His white paws folded over his round, brown body. Sleepy. He felt very light in her arms. That was strange, Dipi thought: when animals become tired, their bodies seem to grow heavier, not lighter. But Freeman was lighter. She gently placed him in the 'coffin' so that she could study him.

The Sergeant interrupted her thoughts. 'Did Mr Fewgitt ever mention going away, Miss?'

'No. I mean, yes.' Dipi's mind was on Freeman. Was he smaller, as well as lighter? Impossible. But the Freeman she stared at *was* smaller. He was the Freeman of a fortnight ago, plumper, rounder, shorter-tailed. She said his name and touched him. At once he came fully awake.

Immediately he did the trick that had pleased her from the very first: he rolled from side to side on his back, front paws floppy, mouth smirking.

'*But he gave up doing that long ago!*' Dipi said to herself. '*He hasn't done that for a week . . . a fortnight!*'

'You haven't answered my question, Miss,' the Sergeant said.

Dipi had other questions in her mind. Questions about Mr Fewgitt. Questions, and their answers . . .

Nelson's blind eye. Mr Fewgitt had said, 'What a genius — and what a fool — that man is!' *Is*, not *was*. Why?

'What work do you do, Mr Fewgitt?'

He had replied, 'My work is to do with having the time of my life.' Why?

'I really must find the right time,' he'd said. 'Just the right time, that is all. Like your parents' right *place*.' Why?

Suddenly the answers were as obvious as the simple mystery of Freeman. Freeman seemed younger because he really was younger; and that was because he had travelled just a short way along the route of Mr Fewgitt's away break.

But Mr Fewgitt had thought of Dipi's fondness for the puppy — halted his journey — left Freeman as a parting gift — then continued on the way to his destination.

'You still haven't answered me, Miss,' said the Sergeant. 'I asked you if Mr Fewgitt ever mentioned going away.'

'Oh, sorry,' Dipi answered. 'I was miles away, thinking about him. Yes, he did say something about taking an away break. He mentioned it the day before all this happened.'

'Did he say where he might be off to? Did he name any particular place?'

'No particular *place*,' Dipi said. Giving this half-truthful answer made her feel one-up on the Sergeant.

He must have noticed her smug look because he said, very seriously, 'You know, Miss, you owe it to him to give any help you can. The old gentleman has gone missing, hasn't he? In suspicious circumstances.'

'I think he just went off to have a — to have a good time,' Dipi said, once again feeling she had made a clever answer.

'I only hope,' the Sergeant said, 'that he hasn't come to a sticky end. Don't you?'

His words shook Dipi, especially the word 'end'. It had not struck her till now that this really was the end. She would never, she knew, see Mr Fewgitt again. Never drink tea with him, never make elaborate jokes about the 'wild beasts', never hear his thin, careful voice. The end.

You would have thought he would have left a proper goodbye, a last message . . .

Perhaps he did! Dipi began an uneasy search. She wandered about the room, apparently aimlessly, her eyes taking in everything. She felt the Sergeant's eyes following her.

'Looking for something?' he said at last.

'Oh — yes — this!' Dipi lied. The golden lump happened to be in front of her. She showed it to the Sergeant. 'Iron pyrites, fool's gold,' she told him.

'Ah yes, Miss. Very pretty.'

Then she spotted the letter. The golden lump had been holding it down. She held out the lump to fix the Sergeant's eye and with her other hand slipped the letter into the pocket of her anorak. 'We used to joke about how rich I would be if it were real gold,' she told the Sergeant.

'So it's yours, Miss?'

'Oh yes. It's mine,' Dipi lied, not quite knowing why she lied.

'Better take it, Miss,' the Sergeant said. 'Everything of his will be under lock and key during our investigations.'

'Oh, I see. Well, can I go now? I can? Good.' She was glad to get away. She wanted to be alone to read Mr Fewgitt's letter.

The letter read:

My dear young friend,

I could hardly hope that you, who display all the Graces and Charms of your sex, do not also possess the female attributes of Curiosity and Cunning. Almost certainly you are by now possessed of my secret; you have doubtless divined that I am a wayfarer along the tracks of *Time*. Other men journey from place to place; I, from time to time.

All journeys must have an end. The end of mine is, I think and hope, at hand. My time must have a stop. Though able to confuse Father Time by hopping like a cricket from century to century, I am now too tired and above all too old to journey on.

I have chosen as my final destination that period of English history when even the humbler gravestones in the Parish churchyard displayed a certain Grace; and when the larger affairs of the nation were proceeding to a climax of excitement and Glory. Nelson's time, dear child! Your Period of history could never be mine. I remained within it as long as I did only because of the happy accident of your delightful presence.

Permit me to thank you for the gift of your company — and to remind you that while 'all that glisters is not Gold', something may be gained by putting this familiar paperweight to the Assayer's acid test.

I kiss your hand and remain,
your devoted Friend,

Tempus Fewgitt

The careful wording and awful typing of the letter made Dipi cry. When she dried her eyes and recovered, the word 'Assayer' made her reach for her dictionary, which told her that an Assayer is one who puts a price on things of value, particularly precious metals. Next day, Dipi took the golden lump to the local jeweller and Assayer.

'Oh, *that*!' he said, tumbling the gold lump from hand to hand. 'Iron pyrites, that is. I suppose you thought it was pure gold? If it was, you'd be a very rich young lady indeed, my goodness me yes!'

'If you'd just *test* it,' Dipi said coldly. She thought the jeweller a nasty little man, pleased with himself for no reason. 'You use an acid, or something, don't you?'

'Waste of my time and yours,' said the jeweller.

'I'll pay you,' Dipi said. She held up a pound. The jeweller shrugged and went to the back of his premises.

When he returned, he was like a fish: his eyes goggled and his mouth gaped. 'It's gold!' he cried. 'It's nearly all gold! Lots of muck, too — but *gold*! It's impossible!'

'What is it worth?' Dipi said.

'Well, I can't tell you *that*, straight *off* . . . Thousands of pounds, obviously. Look, I'll have to charge you on a percentage-of-value basis —'

'Here's your pound,' Dipi said. She handed him the coin, took the golden lump and walked out of the shop.

It was surprising how quickly everything

died down. The broken glass from the basement windows was swept away. The windows were boarded up. The noise of the early morning explosion faded from people's minds. So did the memory of the strange old man. A 'TO LET' board went up. A young couple moved in. The Police Sergeant found a dozen other cases needed attention.

Three things remained: the golden lump, Freeman the puppy, and Dipi's memories.

At first Dipi's parents were scared of the golden lump. 'They'll ask how we got it!' they moaned. 'They'll want us to pay tax — VAT — Treasure Trove!' But then a cousin paid them a visit. He travelled everywhere and knew everything. Somehow the golden lump became a family fortune stashed away in several banks. Somehow the little shop became a chain of shops and Dipi's father happily took up golf and gardening, while Dipi's mother lectured on Indian cookery. She used real saffron instead of turmeric in her *pilau* dishes. Real saffron costs real money.

Freeman the puppy became Freeman the dog — and Dipi's dearest friend.

Dipi's memories stayed as bright as the

golden lump. The lump was not visible and Mr Fewgitt was not visible; but both were still there in one way or another. Dipi could still see his face and say, 'God bless you, Mr Fewgitt,' when she turned out the light to go to sleep in her newly decorated bedroom. 'Goodnight, wherever you are,' she yawned. 'No, that's wrong — *whenever*.'

The Police Sergeant made his last visit. 'We're closing the files on this case,' he told Dipi. 'Closing them officially. Mind you, I'm still curious personally. I get the feeling there's more to Mr Fewgitt's disappearance than meets the eye. And you know more than you've told me. Come, now! What *did* happen?'

'You really want to know, Sergeant?'

'I most certainly do.'

'Then I'll tell you,' Dipi answered, 'some other time.'

In speaking those three words, she spoke the exact truth.

Ghost Alarm

The boy — Leo didn't even know his name — stuck his face close to Leo's and jeered, 'What, you're living in Old Farm? Your Dad must be barmy, taking that place! It's haunted! Spooked!' He pulled a horrible face and waved his arms, imitating a ghost.

'Spooked!' said another boy, crossing his eyes and sticking out his tongue. 'Always has been! For centuries!' This boy's name was Russ, Leo knew. So far, Leo could name only about half the children in his new school. This did not worry him. At the age of eleven, he had been to half a dozen schools. His father's job took him all over the place: when he moved, the family upped sticks and followed.

A girl called Sharon joined in. 'The family that had Old Farm before you,' she said, 'I knew them. They didn't last long. They *saw things* ... !' She shuddered exaggeratedly and rolled her eyes.

'I don't believe in ghosts,' Leo said, flatly. 'Ghosts are for kids.' He pushed through, got his bike from the racks and pedalled steadily through the crowd in the playground. He headed for home. Old Farm. As he rode, he thought, 'You liar! You do believe in ghosts. You're scared stiff of them. Because of the burglar alarm.'

The burglar alarm ...

His father, Mike Winters, had installed it himself. He was an electronics engineer. Alarm systems were child's play to him. So he got busy putting pressure pads under carpets — mounting little projectors that put out invisible beams — building, for the living room, a thing like a loudspeaker cabinet that screamed, deafeningly, if you crossed its path. He enjoyed the job. So did Leo, who helped him.

And so did little Emma, Leo's sister. She trotted about offering the wrong tools at the wrong time. '*Scoo*-driver,' she said, when you needed pliers. '*Why*-ah!' she announced, when you particularly didn't want wire.

Each time her father gravely said, 'Why, thank you, Emma!' and took whatever it was she offered. She was only three.

Then the alarm system was all done and it all worked. The tests had been faultless. 'Walk through it, Kath,' Mike told his wife. She walked, bells rang. 'Come towards me, Emma!' Emma earnestly walked and the loudspeaker cabinet alarm bellowed its head off. Leo and Mike smiled smugly.

Kathy said, 'Look, Mike, we'll all die of heart failure if those things are going to go off every time we make a move.'

'But Kathy, don't you see! — you never *will* hear them. Not unless we get intruders. That's the whole idea.' He made a sidelong face at Leo — a face that meant, '*Women . . .*'

Leo said, 'Honestly, Mum. Never a sound.'

He and his father couldn't have been

more mistaken.

That very night, in the pitch darkness, bells rang and the siren yelled.

Shocked out of sleep, everyone leapt out of bed. Mike said, 'Stay back!' and ran down the staircase. He gripped an ebony club in his hand, a wicked weapon he had picked up in Africa. Leo shone his powerful spotlamp out of an upstairs window. The spot scanned empty fields. Kathy clutched Emma to her. The house seemed to shake with the noise of the alarms.

They found nothing and nobody. No burglars, no ghosts, no intruders. And, in the morning, not a trace of them outside: no damaged window frames, no footsteps in the soft earth.

Mike left early for the airport and a plane to France. Leo went to school. Kathy and Emma were alone in the house . . .

The alarms went off. First, at eleven in the morning. 'Impossible,' Kathy said. 'They're set to work only at night.' She switched off the din.

They went off again in the afternoon. Twice. The second time, Kathy burst into tears, driven to distraction by the awful, head-bursting noise. Emma consoled her and she soon recovered.

Leo came back from school and checked everything. All was in order, yet the alarms had gone off. How was that possible? He thought of ghosts, and shivered.

That night, the alarms went off four times. Leo pushed the cancel button and, holding his father's ebony club, gritted his teeth and looked for intruders. After the third false alarm, Kathy brandished a pair of scissors and shouted, 'Enough! I'm going to cut the wires!'

'For Heaven's sake don't!' Leo cried. 'The system's tamper-proof! Cut the wires and it will go on for ever!' Kathy, white-faced and shaken, went to bed.

Leo, making a final check, heard a small noise — turned — and saw Emma, standing behind him in her nightie. 'Burglar,' she said. 'Over there!' She pointed her finger at the place where the loudspeaker alarm stood.

Leo's spine iced. The lights were on in the living room yet he could see nothing. 'Where? Where?' he shouted.

'Gone now,' Emma said, calmly.

'Why, you little . . . !' Leo began. He almost wanted to brain her with the club. 'If you think that's funny!' he said.

'He was over there,' Emma said, wide-eyed and serious. She pointed to the same place.

Leo swallowed his anger and made tea. Emma silently got the mugs. She said, 'I did see the burglar. I really did.'

'You didn't. You're just a little show-off liar.'

She wasn't listening. 'I thought burglars was robber men,' she said. 'I thought they was people, like us.'

'They are. Here, take this up to Mum and don't spill it.'

At the door she turned and said, 'Our burglar isn't a robber man. He's not proper. He's like glass. And no clothes on. Just glass, and milky.' She was on her dignity.

Leo thought of ghosts. And again shivered.

During the next day the alarm went off twice in the day. Kathy rang a neighbour and asked about local hotels.

In the night it went off three times. The family gave up all hope of sleep. They

78

dozed in the living room. Emma kept looking at the place where the loudspeaker alarm stood.

When the third false alarm sounded, Kathy said, 'I can't stand it! I just can't! We're leaving, I'll call a taxi . . .'

Emma said, 'We can't leave the poor burglar. He's lost. He told me so. He wants to go home . . .'

'Don't, Emma. I'm not in the mood for fairy stories. Just do as you're told.'

'He's only little, he's not much bigger than me. I've seen him three times, four times. Over there. He's lost . . .'

Kathy grabbed Emma's shoulders and started shaking her. Then the alarm went off yet again and Kathy began screaming, holding Emma to her. Emma only half noticed what her mother was doing. Her eyes were fixed on something, or nothing, a little way away.

'It's all right,' she murmured to this thing. 'I've got an idea. *Father Christmas.*'

Leo packed his own suitcase, then helped Kathy pack hers. Her hands were trembling, even her face trembled. 'We're leaving,' she kept saying. 'Getting out.

Quitting.'

In the living room, Emma talked wordlessly with the 'burglar'. Following its instructions, she carefully freed the wires leading to the loudspeaker alarm from the skirting boards. This done, she carried the speaker to the fireplace with its wires attached. It was heavy work for her. Her face was pink.

She placed the cabinet in the fireplace, face up. Getting it positioned just right took her some time but she persevered. When she finished, she nodded and said, 'Father Christmas!' She waited for an answer — apparently got it — and said, 'Yes, that's right. He'll come.'

Father Christmas, she knew, was what the burglar needed. Father Christmas was waiting, just as he waited for her list of Christmas presents, above the chimney. You wrote your list with Mum's help; set fire to it; and Father Christmas somehow read the sparks. Then you got your presents.

It worked for Emma: it would work for the burglar. The burglar wanted to send a message to somewhere up in the sky. Now he could. Father Christmas would hear him.

'All done,' she told the burglar. She knew he understood for he reached out to her — stretched out his glassy, milky limbs. He was sort of under-watery, Emma thought, moving so slowly and feebly. More like a ghost than a burglar. She put out her plump little hand as if to stroke the thing. It was very close to her now, much closer than ever before . . .

The burglar alarm sounded. The noise was awful, Emma had to shield her ears with her hands. The alarm in the fireplace was the worst . . .

And then her mother was rushing down the stairs screaming, 'Out! Get out! I can't stand any more! We'll meet the taxi along the road, get out!' Emma found herself being pulled along like one of the suitcases, dragged along by her mother in the damp night, down the road.

In the house the alarms jangled and screeched and howled. The loudspeaker alarm in the fireplace sent one particular frequency of its noise straight up into the sky — a scream that arrowed through Earth's atmosphere, speared into outer space.

The spaceship picked up the signal. 'Ah!'

said its Commander — a fragile, glassy, milky being with many limbs — 'Ah! We've found him at last!'

In the road near Old Farm, the taxi arrived. Over Old Farm, the spaceship descended. It was glassy, milky, ghostly. It hovered long enough to pick up the crew-member lost for two Earth centuries. It rose, slowly at first but then so fast that clouds were torn to rags.

Only Emma saw it come and go. Only she had been expecting it, or something like it. She looked out of the back window of the taxi, saw the clouds tear and swirl, then heal themselves. She waved and bounced up and down on the seat.

'The burglar's gone,' she said. 'He's gone away so we can go back.' The others ignored her. She tried another tack. 'Suppose Dad telephones,' she said loudly, 'and nobody answers because we're all gone!'

Her mother gasped. 'Oh, I hadn't thought of that! He'd think — I don't know what he'd think! Driver, turn round, take us back!'

These days, no one talks of the Old Farm ghost. The white-painted windows twinkle, the roses Kathy planted flourish. The old house is bright, welcoming, unghostly. Mike refuses to work abroad. He likes his home.

The burglar alarm is still in circuit. Mike brushes the dust off it now and then and tests it. It always works perfectly.

Leo is becoming seriously interested in electronics. Ghosts aren't his thing.

And Emma? Nobody really believed her talk of spaceships and ghosts. Not even her. She is five now. Next month she is going to her first school. It is all she thinks about.

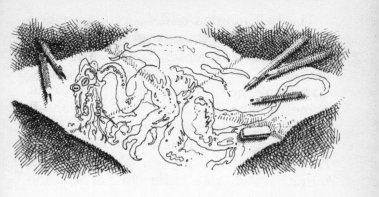

Brainblaster

Mrs Winsor, Head of English for Mick's class, stopped reading, closed the book and said, 'Right. You know what I want you all to do — carry on from where I've stopped in the Class Reader. Obviously the writer is about to bring into the story a threat, a menace — a terrifying being of some sort. A monster, I want you to decide what sort of monster it is: to continue the story in your own way, with your own description of the monster. With drawings, if you like. Understood? Fine. Use your imaginations! See if you can beat the book's author!'

The bell jangled and everyone pushed and shoved and thundered into the open air. School was over for the day. Mick met his sister Polly at the school gates. Together they started the short walk home. 'Pushover!' Mick said. 'I wish all homework were like this: invent a monster. I can invent monsters just like *that*.' He snapped his fingers. 'A monster a minute, each one different, every one guaranteed,' he said.

'But you can't draw them,' Polly said. 'I'm a better drawer than anyone. Pictures stuck up on the classroom walls, and everything.'

'Oh, you're a brill artist, I'll give you that,' said Mick. 'But I'm the word king. Tell you what: I'll do the words and you draw what I tell you.'

'I'll do my own, thank you very much!' Polly began. But then they were home, and tea was waiting, and TV.

Mick watched the telly without seeing it. His mind was full of monsters. Polly was the same. 'That's feeble!' she said, when the badly drawn cartoon monster on the TV jerkily reared up and tried to look frightening. 'Pathetic!' she said, when the space-suited humans cried, 'Oh, my *garsh*!' and 'Hully gee, this could be curtains!'

'Let's see you do better,' Mick said.

'All right. Just watch.' She turned her back on the TV and started drawing on a big sketch pad. She drew fast and well.

Soon Mick too forgot the TV and watched her sketch grow. 'That's great!' he said. 'Now give him fangs, dripping fangs! . . . That's it, great!'

The telly, ignored, shouted, 'This is *turrible*!' and 'Somebuddy *help* me!' Polly kept on drawing. Mick scribbled words. The tea never got drunk.

They were still young enough to be sent to bed quite early, but bedtime made little difference to Mick and Polly. In their bedrooms they just went on doing whatever they were doing while their parents yawned in front of the TV.

This evening they got on with their monster.

It got better by the minute. He — she — it — started out as a more or less standard monster, with glaring eyes, a snarling, fire-breathing mouth and a scaly tail. But Polly really could draw and Mick really

87

did have imagination. By ten o'clock their monster was coming alive.

It was not too big: as Mick said, 'I'm sick of king-size monsters towering over cities and tearing up electric pylons. A really scarey monster would just about fill a room . . . a room with *you* in it, *alone!*'

And their monster wasn't covered with scales and knobs. As Polly said, 'I want it sort of slithery and oily — but with huge muscles under the slither. Touching it would make you feel sick!'

Their parents came up to prepare for bed. 'You two!' their father called out, 'you're supposed to be *asleep*. In your own rooms and your own beds. Come on, now!' They obeyed. But as soon as the parents' bedroom door was closed, Mick crept back to Polly's room. There, by the shaded light of a bedside lamp, they got on with their monster.

Next day Mick handed in homework to Mrs Winsor. He couldn't resist including Polly's drawing of the monster.

The day after, she gave back all the written work, marked. Mick got top marks and also a 'Vg!', meaning Very Good. Mrs Winsor wrote 'Brilliant!' on

Polly's drawing. So Mick and Polly were very pleased with themselves.

Yet when school was over, Mrs Winsor pounced on the two of them by the school gates. She said, 'I want a word with you two.' She did not look as if she were about to congratulate them. In fact, she looked almost cross.

'That drawing of yours, Polly,' she said.

'Yes, Mrs Winsor? You mean this?' Polly held out the monster drawing.

'That's the one,' said Mrs Winsor, frowning.

'I haven't got the eyes quite right yet,' Polly said. 'What do you think?' She held the drawing closer to Mrs Winsor's face. But Mrs Winsor didn't seem to want to look at it. Indeed, she appeared to want *not* to look at it.

'You gave me a 'Vg' too,' Mick said, not wanting to be left out.

'You deserved it,' said Mrs Winsor. 'Both of you. So much effort. I don't know how you found the time to be so — so thorough . . . to make such a complete job of it.'

'Oh, we haven't finished yet,' Polly said.

'I think you've done enough,' said Mrs

Winsor.

'But some things aren't quite right,' Polly began.

'No, you've done enough. Quite enough,' said Mrs Winsor, almost angrily. Then, 'Well . . . congratulations, both of you.' She left them.

Polly and Mick began walking home. Mick said, 'What was all that about?'

'Search me! Perhaps she's going psychoceramic. Crackpot.'

Mick said, 'But she's not the crackpot type. She's OK, for a teacher.'

'Perhaps our monster frightened her,' Polly said. She opened up the drawing and looked at it as she walked. 'It really is scarey,' she said. 'Almost alive.'

'That's my super-brill writing. All my brilliant ideas. And I've got lots more. Listen, Poll: it doesn't just chew up *bodies* and all that: it's a *mind*-eater, see? Goes for your brains, get it?'

'Of course I get it,' Polly said. 'That's the way I've drawn it. That's why it's so frightening. You can see it wants to slither into your mind and take over —'

'No, it *starts* in your brain, then bursts out.'

'Same difference,' Polly said. She

added, 'I've got to do more to the eyes . . .
You talk, and I'll draw what you say.' She
licked her lips, looking forward to the
work.

They did not finish Brainblaster — that
was the name they gave their monster —
until two midnights later. He took so long
because he constantly improved. When at
last he was done, he was a masterpiece of
ideas and images; and Polly and Mick
were exhausted.

'My eyes feel as if they'd been sand-
papered,' Mick said. 'I'm packing it in,
Poll. Bed.'

'Help me clear up first,' Polly said. Very
quietly, they put felt pens, brushes,
colours and everything else away. Mick
dropped a bottle of ink. It went down with
what seemed an enormous crash, but
neither parent rushed in saying, 'What
was that? What are you up to?'

'Now, sleep!' Polly said. 'Sleep, sleep,
sleep . . . But at least we've finished
Brainblaster.' She couldn't keep her eyes
off the drawing. But she could barely keep
them open, either.

'Finished and fantastic,' Mick said.
'Brill, skill, sooper-de-luxe, terrifico.'

He went to his bedroom and slept instantly.

Polly was asleep almost before her head touched the pillow.

On the floor, lit by the faint glow of the street lamp outside Polly's window, Brainblaster seemed wide awake. His wicked eyes glared from the dull whiteness of the paper. His dripping mouth leered open and ready. The layered muscles seemed to flex and strain beneath the oily glistening hide . . .

The little bedroom should have burst like a blown-up paper bag when Brainblaster exploded into life, his serpent eyes blazing red fire, his vampire wings like a devil's cloak, his fanged mouth spewing yellow venom as the raw skull swivelled on the vulture neck!

The monster uttered; and his voice was the thunderclap that rattles tiles from the roof — the screech of metal against metal as trains collide — the trumpeting howl of a bull elephant trapped in a pit — the cackling scream of witches as the great cauldron froths and boils, tumbling its hideous contents in the surging scum.

In his bedroom, rigid as a corpse, his heart clogging his throat, Mick tried to scream and could not.

In her bedroom, her skin frozen with fear, her hands like white claws, Polly tried to shrink back — to shout — to do anything, anything at all — and could not.

Brainblaster swung his ridged skull between the peaks of his leathery wings. He filled each room. His wings scraped shelves. The warted hump of his back brushed the ceiling. The slime from his curling lips dropped on Mick's chest, on Polly's outstretched arms —

Dropped, but left no trace! And on the shelves brushed by his wings, familiar objects were left undisturbed. No oily stains from his back marked the ceiling. No one flung open the bedroom doors, crying, 'What's that?'

The monster spoke. 'Sssso . . . !' he said. His vast head loomed still closer to the children's faces. His tongue slithered like a snake's. The glare of his eyes painted the bedclothes with black shadows and red highlights.

'You summoned me,' he said. 'I am come. Sssso . . .?'

At last Polly could speak, in a voice shrivelled with fear. 'Go,' she pleaded. 'Please, please, go!'

At last Mick's pounding heart no longer clogged his throat. 'Go away!' said the ghost of his voice. 'Oh, go away!'

And the monster was gone.

Next day — 'Stop saying it's impossible!' Mick told Polly. 'It happened. To you and me. Separately but together. You know it did.'

'But why didn't it wreck the room — burn the paper off the walls — shatter the windows?' Polly said.

'It didn't *damage* anything because it wasn't *real*!' Mick shouted.

'Then how did it come to life? It was just a drawing and some words —'

'How am *I* supposed to know? Perhaps because it was so perfect. Our invention, I mean.'

'That's it,' Polly whispered. Fear made her whisper, him shout. 'Too perfect. That must be it. Brainblaster is too good *not* to be true! Mrs Winsor saw it. She knew. It's alive.'

'Not *alive*,' Mick blustered. 'It's just — just a projection . . .'

'A projection? From our minds, you mean?'

'Like a transparency from a camera, or something. I don't know, how *can* I know?'

'It won't come back, will it?' Polly whispered.

'Why ask me?' Mick shouted. Then, see-ing his sister's face, and remembering that she was younger than he — only nine — he said, 'I shouldn't think so. And any-way, I've got an idea.'

'What?'

'Well, if it's only a projection . . . look, I can't explain now. But tell you what, I'll

sleep in your room tonight. On the floor.
Then you won't be alone.

'Just in case,' Polly said.

'That's right. Just in case.'

In the middle of the night Brainblaster
returned; exploded into life with a thun-
dering roar that should have roused the
neighbourhood; with a shattering presence that should have cracked the walls;
with a dark glow of evil that should have
frozen heart and mind.

'Sssso . . . !' he breathed with a breath
like foul fire. 'You summoned me. I am
come!'

'We didn't summon you,' Mick managed to say.

'I am come. Sssso. . . .?'

'Go away!' Polly howled. 'We don't
want you!'

'Oh yes, you want me. You made me.
Sssso?'

'We made you all wrong,' Mick said.
'Everything about you is wrong. You're a
mistake! To begin with, you're the wrong
size, we didn't want you that big —'

'Sssso?'

'Be smaller,' Polly said. 'Much smaller.'

The monster made a sound that could

have been a laugh — a thunderous cackle that hurt the ear. 'Sssso!' it said; and shrank.

'Smaller still!' Polly said.

It shrank to the size of a bat. Polly gave a gasp of relief. But then it crouched — sprang upwards — and began flying.

Polly seized Mick's arm with fingers like pincers. 'Horrible!' she said, and hid her face in his shoulder so as not to see the hideous thing circling the room, wavering, darting, threatening to brush against her, to catch in her hair. 'Keep it away from me!' she screamed. 'Don't let it touch me!'

Mick made himself watch the leathery wings, the waving rat tail, the malicious, luminous eyes. 'Let go of me, Poll! I've got to use my hands!' Brainblaster still circled the room. His wings made secretive, rustling sounds. The wicked head strained on the vulture neck. Mick stood in the centre of the room, shoulders tensed, arms outspread, turning his body to follow the monster's flight. Then —

'Got you!' he cried as his hands snapped the lid over the neck of the glass jar and screwed the lid down.

They watched the trapped thing in its

prison. Its claws slid against the glass walls, making high, tiny, scratching noises. Its jaws gaped and snapped. The snake tongue darted in and out of the yellow-roofed mouth; the hollow fangs leaked greenish venom.

'Got you,' Mick repeated in a savage murmur.

Brainblaster gave a hideous grin, spat venom — and disappeared.

The glass jar was empty.

'It won't come back, will it?' Polly said.

'Course not. Gone. Done. Finished. End of Brainblaster.'

'You're sure? Really sure?'

'Even if he came back, what would it matter? I mean, we know about him now. He's nothing real. He's just what I said — a projection.'

He held the empty jar up to the light of the window. 'See for yourself!' he told Polly. 'Empty! Nobody home!'

'Don't let it come back, ever!' Polly said in a whisper.

But Brainblaster did come back. Often. When Polly and Mick were asleep there might be the slightest rattling sound from the place where the jar was kept, on the shelf by the window. The sound was the glass jar shaking. There might be a moving glow from a furious pair of eyes: the monster's eyes. There might be squeaks and scrapings as claws and fangs scratched at the smooth glass.

But sleepers' ears hear nothing and sleepers' eyes are blind.

Weeks later, Mrs Winsor said, 'Hello, Polly. I've been thinking about you and your art work. Your art teacher showed me your flower drawings.'

'What, these, Mrs Winsor? The anenomes?'

'Oh, you've got them with you, have you? I think I know why! They're being shown to the whole Lower School this afternoon, aren't they? Through the epidiascope.'

'Yes, that's right. But they don't look the same when they're projected. All the faults show up.'

All the same, you must be very pleased with yourself, Polly. You certainly should be. You get such life into your drawings.'

'Thank you, Mrs Winsor.'

'Oh, another thing, Polly —'

'Yes, Mrs Winsor?'

'Oh, nothing really. I suddenly remembered a drawing of yours that I *didn't* like. A sort of monster you did.'

'We burned it, Mrs Winsor. Yonks ago. Me and Mick.'

Mrs Winsor had seemed uneasy. Now she was herself again. 'You burned it?' she said. 'Oh. Well, I'm glad. There was something about it that I . . . something that I . . .'

'Yes, Mrs Winsor?'

'Well, whatever you do, don't burn the flower drawings, Polly. They're something to be proud of!'

'Thank you, Mrs Winsor.'

A boiling summer day. Brilliant sunshine from a cloudless sky. Brainblaster decides to reappear. His trick of vanishing, he has learned, means nothing: for vanishing is not escaping. He is still imprisoned in the glass jar. He has tried time and again to escape into the darkness of night — and always failed. Now he will try the light of day.

The glass jar is almost forgotten now. It has been knocked over. It lies on its side on the shelf by the window. The sun strikes the glass at an angle, warming it.

The jar is a strong one. Its thick base is doubly curved, rather like a lens.

The sun shines ever brighter and stronger. Morning gives way to afternoon. The sun curves across the sky. Now its rays are almost in line with the tube formed by the walls of the glass jar. The glass glows and gleams and its reflections twinkle on wall and ceiling.

Afternoon gives way to early evening. The sun is lower in the sky, but it is still a marvellous day, a brilliant day. And the sun's rays keep their power.

And now the rays of the sun are almost exactly in line with the axis of the glass jar. It is bathed in light but shadowed in the centre by a dark shape: the tense, crouched shape of Brainblaster.

To make a projection, you must have a projector. To make a projector, you need only a strong light to illuminate the object or image; and a lens.

Now the sun's rays are exactly in line with the jar. See how the glass floods with light!

And do you notice how the light is collected by the lens-like base of the jar? — collected, focused, then flung, hugely magnified, on to the whiteness of that inner wall?

And do you see that great, dark, furiously moving shape in the centre of that disc of light?

A sudden leap — a triumphant howl — and the dark shape is gone from the disc.

Brainblaster is free again.

One Is One and All Alone

Dear Diary,

I get so lonely, that's my trouble. I am the only child on this ship. Everyone else is a grown-up, with things to do. They're all busy running the ship or checking their equipment for when we land on Trion.

Yes, we're heading for Trion! Isn't that exciting? No, it's not. Not exciting at all.

When we set out I used to tick off the days on my calendar. We left Earth on March 12 2045. So I ticked off March 12, 13, 14, 15 ... Then April ... May ... June. Then I gave up. We don't reach Trion until mid-January 2047. By then

I'll be eleven. Eleven! Isn't that exciting? No, it's not. I'll still be the same old Trish, but bigger and older.

Dad does his best, he's always poking his head round the door, grinning at me. 'How's things? Everything all right? How about you and me meeting in the diner at six for a chocolate whip?'

I grin back and say, 'Yum, yum!' but even as I say it his face changes, the grin is still there but the busy look is back in his eyes: there are a thousand things in his mind. After all, he's the ship's Executive Officer, a big man. Even when he talks to you he's glancing sideways at the latest printouts.

And I suppose he misses Mum as much as I do. Almost as much, anyhow. She's on Trion, helping set up the base and everything. Busy Dad, busy Mum.

Which leaves me all alone in front of my VoicePrinter, talking to it, talking and talking. Then I watch it print out what I've been saying, my private diary. It corrects my spelling and punctuation. It's clever. I can switch it from Diary to Dialogue — from Graphics to Constructs. For instance, I've taught it to make jungles for me, full of animals leaping about. And it has taught me games and lessons. I suppose it's my best friend, really. Let's switch from Diary to Dialogue and find out . . .

ARE YOU MY BEST FRIEND, VP?

    I HOPE I AM, I TRY TO BE. BUT LATER, ON TRION, YOU WILL MEET HUMAN COMPANIONS: BOYS AND GIRLS LIKE YOURSELF.

NOT FOR A LONG TIME, VP.

    WE MUST BE PATIENT. MEANTIME, I AM YOUR TRUE FRIEND. SHALL WE PLAY A GAME? POP STAR! SHALL WE PLAY THAT?

OK, VP. DO A CONSTRUCT FOR ME, A REALLY GOOD ONE. LET'S HAVE A HEAVY DRUM ROLL, THEN I MAKE MY ENTRANCE THROUGH CLOUDS OF COLOURED SMOKE. I'D LIKE A BIG SWINGING CHAIN ROUND MY NECK.

    THIS OK?

GREAT. RIGHT, HERE I COME, THROUGH THE SMOKE ... TWO, THREE, FOUR — ACTION!

I begin singing and the other Me, the pop star on VP's enormous screen, acts out being a pop star. VP has made me taller and older, about seventeen. VP is terrific on Constructs.

    Exciting, isn't it! No, it's not.

    I'm sick of Me, sick of being the ship's

Only Child, sick of computer images and sounds. If only I had someone to talk to, to be with! Someone of my age . . .

YOU KNOW WHAT I MEAN, DON'T YOU, VP?

OF COURSE I DO. I SYMPATHIZE. SHALL WE PLAY SOMETHING ELSE?

NO, LET'S NOT PLAY ANY MORE. TEACH ME SOMETHING. WHERE DID WE GET TO LAST LESSON?

WE REACHED 'CLO'. SO I TAUGHT YOU ABOUT CLOCKS.

WHAT FOLLOWS CLOCKS?

CLONE. C-L-O-N-E. CLONES AND CLONING.

TEACH ME ABOUT CLONES AND CLONING, THEN.

CERTAINLY. A CLONE IS THE EXACT REPRODUCTION OF A LIVING THING MADE BY TAKING A SMALL PART OF THE ORIGINAL — A SCRAP OF TISSUE, SAY — AND USING THIS SCRAP AS THE PATTERN FROM WHICH A DUPLICATE OF THE ORIGINAL IS CREATED.

OH DEAR! . . . NO, WAIT, I REMEMBER NOW. THEY CLONED FROGS IN THE LAST CENTURY, DIDN'T THEY?

FROGS AND MANY OTHER ANIMALS.

THAT'S RIGHT — THEY TOOK A TINY SCRAPING FROM THE FROG'S SKIN AND SORT OF BREWED UP HUNDREDS OF FROGS FROM THAT LITTLE SCRAPING?

QUITE SO. AND ALL THE FROGS WERE IDENTICAL BECAUSE ALL WERE CONSTRUCTED FROM THE SAME ORIGINAL TO THE SAME PATTERN.

I BET IT WAS COMPLICATED!

IT WAS. IT IS.

CERTAINLY. WHY, THE RESOURCES
AVAILABLE IN THIS SHIP'S BIOLAB
WOULD BE SUFFICIENT TO SET UP A
CLONE LABORATORY. YOU SEE, ALL
THAT IS REQUIRED...

VP went on and on describing cloning
techniques. I paid no attention because I
was thinking, very hard. But I made sure
to record VP's words.

I'll tell you what I was thinking. The
BioLab in this ship is very big. It has to
be, because biology is what this trip is all
about: the biology of Trion — what lives
there now, what and who could live there
in the future.

At this moment the ship's BioLab is
deserted. It won't become busy until we
reach Trion.

I need to use it.

I need it all to myself.

I will make a clone. It will be my perfect
friend and companion.

Perfect, because I am going to clone
myself. Make another Me.

Dear Diary,

I haven't spoken to you for ages
because I've been so busy with my new
friend, Clo.

Clo for 'Clone'.

Clo is me. I am Clo. We are identical

twins. No, even closer than that. Clo is made *of* me, *from* me. We are one.

Except that there are two of us! — which is tricky. I mean, suppose Dad put his head round the door and saw two Trishes instead of one!

But I've solved that. My cabin door leads to an identical cabin next door. Clo can vanish through that door like a ghost, in a split second. The next-door cabin is empty, of course — all the cabins are: they won't be filled until the return trip from Trion. So I sleep here, Clo sleeps there. Clothes, food, toothbrushes? Well, yes, I now need two of everything — but the ship is loaded with stores, nobody notices or cares about an extra toothbrush, an extra towel.

In fact, everything's fine as long as we don't both appear in the same place at the same time! We simply arrange *not* to. Though, just the other night, we nearly made a big mistake . . .

In the middle of the night I had to go to the loo. It's just down the corridor. I got out of bed, opened the door — and met myself, face to face! For there was Clo. We stared at each other, eyes and mouths wide open, then burst into identical giggles.

Which all goes to show how identical we are. We even get the urge to go to the loo at the same time!

No wonder we're such perfect friends.

Dear Diary,

Once again, it's been a long time since I made an entry. There have been so many things on my mind.

The truth is, Clo can be a bit of a pain sometimes. Only in small ways, nothing serious. But this *picking* habit . . . When

Clo has nothing to do, it's always pick, pick, pick. Rolling bits of skin around a fingernail. You can't avoid looking at the fingers, they writhe and fiddle all the time. Pick, pick, *pick*.

The other evening, I'd had enough. I gave Clo a good old glare and said, loudly and plainly, 'Look — do you *mind*? Stop picking at yourself!'

You'll never believe it, but at the very moment I said those words, Clo glared at me and said, 'Look — do you *mind*? Stop picking at yourself!'

Me, a picker! I never pick at my fingers. Those tiny little bits of frayed skin — well, they just happen naturally; everyone's got them.

I can't stand people who pick.

Dear Diary,

Long time no see, but here I am again talking to dear old VP, my only true friend.

Clo is in the other cabin, having a sulk-in. It's always sulks these days and they always start the same way . . .

'Don't keep *repeating* me!'

'I wasn't repeating you, I spoke first!'

'You didn't. I did.'

'Well, even if I didn't say it first, I *thought* it first. I can't even have my

110

thoughts to myself, you're always butting in and — and — interrupting my train of thought!'

'Interrupting my train of thought!'

So we even use the same words at the same time.

At first it was a joke. We'd catch ourselves doing it and laugh. But I'm not laughing any more, I can tell you. You don't want to share *everything*: some thoughts are private.

Last night Clo did something I cannot forgive. I was thinking about Mum — I'm always thinking of her — and I suppose I gave a sort of sigh and murmured, 'Oh, Mum . . .'

As I said it, Clo said exactly and precisely the same thing. 'Oh, Mum . . . ' Clo said, and gave a sigh.

Now, that's going too far, don't you agree? I mean, my Mum is *my* Mum, nothing to do with Clo. *My* Mum, mine only.

I'm not going to put up with this kind of thing. It's like being swamped, invaded, taken over. You can't even go to Commissary & Stores and pick yourself a pair of new shoes — white shoes with red leather bits, really smart — without finding the *other* person wearing exactly the same shoes.

And crossword puzzles. We don't share the same room, Clo and I, if we can avoid it; so I started doing those old-fashioned crossword puzzles. You do them on your own, with your head down and your mind fully occupied.

Well, how would *you* like it when, after puzzling over a clue for ages, you suddenly find the answer and shout it out — *'NAVIGATOR!'* — and, at that very moment, hear a voice from next door shout, *'NAVIGATOR!'*

And those are only the small things. To be truthful, I can't stand the way Clo's mind works. I can't stand Clo's corny jokes, dismal sulks. I can't stand Clo's laugh or eating habits or finger-picking. And I *won't* stand Clo intruding on my most private and personal thoughts.

One of the features of this ship is its disposal system. There are five big hatches, each one marked *DISPOSAL*. You open the hatch — put the thing you want to get rid of into the hole — and *whoosh*, it's gone. Disposed of for ever into infinite space.

One of the five hatches happens to be just outside my cabin, in the corridor. There's never anyone in the corridor at night.

There you are, then. Tonight's the

night. I'll be disposing of something, definitely. I could even write a note to go with the item to be disposed of. The note would read, 'Goodbye, Clo. Have a good trip. Yours never, Trish.'

Well, it wouldn't be murder, would it? How could it be? You can't be charged with murdering *yourself*, can you? You couldn't even be charged with suicide, because there's still a person left and that person is alive — walking and talking, eating and sleeping.

So it's foolproof. Goodbye, Clo. Yours never, Trish.

Dear Diary,
Over and done with. Finished and forgotten.

No, that's not true! There's no question of *forgetting*. Just the opposite. Every minute of every hour, I mentally hug myself and give a silent shout of 'Whoopee! Yarroop! Hooray! Finally free! Alone at last!'

Even Dad noticed. 'You're looking wonderful today,' he said. 'Suddenly you're bright as a button!'

'I feel terrific,' I said. 'Can I have a chocolate whip?'

'Have as many as you like.'

'Just one,' I said. 'Only *one*.' One's

enough, isn't it? Who needs two? There's only one Me! No longer do I have to remind another Me to wipe chocolate froth from its greedy mouth. No longer do I have to listen to that other Me's corny 'Yum-yum!' noises whenever chocolate whips are mentioned. From now on, there's only one Me. You've no idea how wonderful it feels; how bright the future looks.

Too bad about Trish, of course. 'Down the hatch!' I said. The hatch went *whoosh*. 'Goodbye, Trish,' I said. 'Fond remembrances, I don't think.'

But that's something I must remember from now on — my name. It isn't Clo any more. Now I'm Trish.

Trish, that's me.

Susan's Plant

'No!' said Susan's mother. 'I'm sorry, Susan, but no! They will *not* let you take it. There won't be room. We're allowed only the things on the list — things we must have, like clothes and brushes and shoes. You can't take your plant.'

Now Susan was only six; but she was clever. She *was* going to take her plant with her. The plant grew in a red pot. The flowers were yellow and white and the leaves were bright green. She loved it and she was going to take it with her when she and her mother travelled to Leda 3.

Susan's father was a spaceman. He was a long way away, out there in the sky.

115

Sometimes at night her mother took Susan to her bedroom window and said, 'Look, Susan! There's Leda, can you see it?' Through the telescope, Leda was just a dot of light, nothing more. But Susan's mother said, 'That's where your father is. And that's where we're going!'

'How soon?' Susan always asked.

'Very soon.'

'And we'll be with Daddy, won't we?'

'That's right. With Daddy.'

'Why is he there? Why can't he stay home with us?'

'You know why he's there. To find out if people can live on Leda.'

'It's very small, isn't it?'

'Yes, Leda's very small.'

'But it's nice there, isn't it?'

'Well . . . I think it is. And it will be nice to see Daddy again.'

'I don't care if it's horrible,' Susan said, 'as long as we're with Daddy.'

She looked hard through the telescope, trying to see something more than a dot of light. But that was all there was. A dot .

She said, 'Have they got plants there?'

'Yes, some. I think.'

'Then why can't I take my plant?'

'Now, Susan! I've told you why. Don't be silly.'

Susan said, 'What's Daddy doing up there?'

'He's a sort of manager. I'm going to help him with his work.'

'And me — what will I do?'

'You'll be a good girl. A *very* good girl.'

'How can I be a good girl without my plant?'

'We'll take its red pot. Will that make you happy? I can pack things in the pot, I suppose. O K?'

'Yes,' Susan said to her mother. To herself she said, 'No. I *will* take my plant. I *won't* leave it behind.'

But how would she do it?

She thought and thought until she found the answer.

Susan knew the rules. She would be allowed to take one, single toy in addition to her proper luggage. She decided to take her teddy bear.

She decided on him because he was big and old and soft. You could get at him. Get into him.

Using her mother's scissors, she cut open her teddy. She did it neatly, stitch by stitch. Then she made his stuffing wet. Wet, but not soaking.

Next, she took her plant from its pot, with plenty of soil round the roots; and put the plant inside the bear.

Finally, she packed damp stuffing round the plant and sewed her teddy together again. She did it quite well, really. And even if the stitching looked a bit rough, no one would bother. He was an old, battered bear.

And now it was time to go to the spaceport. Everything was packed and ready. Susan's mother said, 'There's your case, there are my cases, here are the tickets and things . . . ' She had too many things to do. Yet she still noticed Susan's teddy. 'Susan!' she said sharply. 'Your teddy feels wet! What have you been doing to him?'

'Oh, nothing, Mummy! I just gave him a wash to make him look nice for Daddy! That's all!'

'Oh dear, oh Lord!' her mother said. 'I suppose I'll have to put him in a plastic bag . . . Oh dear, you are a nuisance, Susan!'

Susan said nothing. She thought, 'Good! A plastic bag will keep the moisture in. Just right for my plant!'

When they got to Leda, Susan was so happy to see her father that she almost forgot about her bear and the plant inside him. Almost, but not quite. As soon as she was alone she cut the bear open — he was still damp inside — and took out her plant.

It looked awful: limp, crumpled and miserable.

When she put the plant in its red pot, it looked even worse. She touched the floppy leaves and whispered to it. 'Come on!' she said. 'You'll be all right! I'm giving you water, see? Fresh water. Drink it all up! You'll soon feel better!'

But the plant looked as sad as ever. She hid it under her bed and fell asleep worrying about it.

Next day the plant looked hardly any better. It was alive, but only just. Susan tried to forget about it. She would find out about her new home, Leda.

Everyone on the little planet was busy. The people lived in a home unit, sealed off. The spacemen were busy all the time making the air they breathed, the water they drank, the heat, light and power they needed. So the home unit was like a big machine, always giving trouble.

The worst of the troubles for Susan was that there was nowhere to go. 'Can't we go outside and look around?' she asked her father.

'I'm sorry, but no. You've got to stay inside.'

'Why?'

'Because the air outside is no good. It's not like the air at home, on Earth.'

'But I can see people outside! Lots of them!'

'Yes, but they're all wearing special helmets. The helmets feed them air so that they can breathe and live.'

'I'll wear a helmet. Give me a helmet!'

'Sorry, but that's impossible. Your head's too small to fit properly.'

A woman overheard their talk. She said, 'Oh, but Susan must see the place! Tell you what: I'll take her in the helicopter!'

So Susan saw Leda 3 after all. It had low hills and dull-looking seas without waves. Sometimes she saw animals moving about, but not often. When the helicopter landed she thanked the pilot woman and went to her father.

'It's not a very exciting place, is it, Daddy?' she said. 'And everything seems to be the same colour. All the plants are a sort of yellow-green. *My* plant is much nicer!'

'Your plant?' said her father.

'Oh — yes, well — I didn't want anybody to know —'

But very soon her father found out about the plant. He rubbed his chin and looked worried.

'Are you angry, Daddy?'

'No,' her father said. 'I don't think I am. Your plant can't do any harm . . . but it's a good thing it wasn't discovered on the flight!'

The pilot woman said, 'So you cut your teddy bear open, did you, and smuggled the plant in! You little devil!' She laughed. Susan's father laughed.

Susan said, 'It's not funny, it's very serious. My plant isn't well, it could be dying!'

Her father was serious now. He said, 'You're right. If we could find out how to make plants like yours — plants from Earth — stay alive on this planet, half our troubles would be over. If plants lived here, so could we. We'd be able to leave the home unit and breathe the air. As it is, all the plants die. We've tried, but . . . ' He shrugged his shoulders.

The pilot woman said, 'Look out there, Susan. See those people scratching at the soil? They're trying to make a garden, trying to raise crops. We've been trying for a very long time but we never succeed. Everything dies . . . '

Leda was a dull place, but Susan got used to it. She played with her teddy, watched her mother and father working, looked out of the windows and attended to her plant. It did not live and it did not die. It just looked ill.

She looked out of the windows in the hope of seeing the Wrigglepigs. She gave them that name: soon everyone used it. The Wrigglepigs were animals about the size of cats. They were built rather like pigs, but their noses were very long, almost like trunks. Sometimes they did a sort of wriggling dance. Susan claimed that they danced for her the very first time she was close to them, but really she was not sure about this.

In fact, nobody knew much about the

Wrigglepigs. The spacemen had given up trying to make friends with the little animals. As soon as anyone talked to them, they stopped doing whatever they were doing — which, usually, was rooting about with their snouts in the earth — and began instead to wriggle and dance, as if embarrassed. Then they ran away.

'Well, what do you think of them?' Susan's father said.

'Oh, I don't know,' Susan answered. 'They look a bit stupid when they wriggle about like that, but I don't think they're as silly as they make out. They've got clever eyes.'

'Clever eyes?' her father said. He looked at the Wrigglepigs through his binoculars. 'You really think so?' He went on staring in silence.

'Why do they eat like that?' Susan said.

'Like what?'

'They have to look and look for the plants they eat,' Susan said. 'It takes them hours to find their food. And when they've eaten it, they spend more hours just *breathing into the ground*! Look, there's one doing it now! Breathing in and out as hard as he can, with his long nose stuck in the ground! Why?'

Susan's father said, 'You're right. Breathing away like anything. But don't ask me why, I don't know.'

'And, Daddy, some Wrigglepigs never do find food. Can you see that one over there, on your left, lying still?'

'Yes, I've got him.'

'Well, he was there yesterday, lying still, just the same.'

Her father said, 'Don't upset yourself. Come on, we'll find your mother. Perhaps she'll play with you.'

Next day Susan found new people to play with. Some men were making the home unit bigger. They were knocking a hole in a wall. Susan watched them. The men liked her being there. They talked to her about helicopters and homes and holidays.

Soon, Susan became their boss. They put a plastic hat on her head and gave her a long piece of wood with which to wallop them. 'Work harder, you bad men!' Susan shouted.

'Yes, Boss! Sorry, Boss! May we move this trolley, Boss?'

'Yes, but I've got to ride on it. Lift me

up, put me on it. Good. Faster! Faster!'

The men pushed the trolley. Susan whacked them with her strip of wood. The men cried, 'Ow!' and pulled agonized faces. Everyone had such a good time that it seemed almost a pity when the day's work was over.

They did some tidying-up and said, 'Well, that's it. Back again tomorrow.' One man picked up Susan and she rode on his shoulders, her helmet over one eye and her boss stick waving around, whacking away at the laughing men.

The place where they had been working was dark now. The lights were all turned off. But a little patch of light lit the back of a crate that had been pushed against the wall. The light came from outside. There was a hole in the wall, a small gap.

During the night a Wrigglepig put his long nose into the hole and sniffed. Other Wrigglepigs joined him, jostling and sniffing.

They must have liked the smell of the place, for soon the new extension to the home unit was filled with Wrigglepigs.

Susan slept in a very small room, only just big enough for her bed and bedside table. On the table were a light, a glass of water, the helmet the men had given her and her plant. Above the table there was the usual little radio and intercom with the usual little red panic button. Should an emergency arise, you pressed the red button. But Leda 3 was efficiently run. The red buttons were never used.

Susan never used her radio either. If you wanted to listen to music, you kept hearing interruptions — men's voices, women's voices, people making announcements. Susan was quite happy to talk to her teddy bear or her plant. That night, she said to the plant, 'Oh, do come on! You look terrible! Drink this water, get yourself big and strong!' But the plant simply looked sad and droopy. Susan fell asleep worrying about it.

Her sleep was disturbed by noises.

She thought she heard things moving, scuffling. And a sort of 'talking' from high, small voices. She turned over and pulled a pillow over her head, but the noises went on. Sniffings, scufflings, 'talk'.

Then came a noise that she could not ignore — a bump close to her head, a rattle from the bedside table. She groped for the switch of her lamp, switched on the light, and sat up in bed.

What she saw frightened her so much that though she tried to scream — though her mouth was wide open — only a gasping noise came from her.

The room was full of Wrigglepigs.

Their bodies writhed and tumbled over each other. They scrambled, climbed, fell, heaved. One had his snout in her glass of water. The glass overbalanced and made a small crash as it hit the floor. Several Wrigglepigs funnelled up the water through their long noses.

But it was Susan's plant that really interested them. Snouts waved towards the plant — pink-nostrilled, shiny snouts. Plump bodies strained upwards towards it.

'Go away!' Susan screamed. 'Go away, away, *away*!'

At once the Wrigglepigs froze. Silently they gazed at Susan. She was right: their eyes were clever. They looked *knowing*. Then some of them tried to climb up on Susan's bed . . .

Susan shouted. They took no notice. Their blunt paws pulled at the bedclothes, their snouts waved at her, their clever eyes were fixed on her.

Susan sobbed and screamed and pushed the red panic button. The button fell out of its hole.

'Please, please!' Susan cried. 'Tell me what you want! I'm Susan, I'm your friend! Oh, *please*!'

The Wrigglepigs did not listen. They all began to dance, even the ones on her bed. They danced faster and faster. Susan tried to stop her eyes and ears with her hands. 'Stop it!' she screamed. But the Wrigglepigs went on dancing.

Then, as suddenly as they had begun, they stopped. Their 'talk' noises began. They looked at each other and at Susan while they 'talked'. The Wrigglepigs on her bed came even closer to Susan and stared into her eyes. Then they swung their heads to look at the real centre of interest: the plant; Susan's plant.

The door was flung open and Susan's mother was there. Her face was white. 'Susan! — Susan! —'

'Oh, Mother, make them stop! They've broken my plant and they've been dancing and they stare at me —'

'I'll call everyone,' her mother said. She reached for the panic button.

'It's no good,' Susan wailed. 'It's broken!'

Susan's mother looked for something with which to hit the Wrigglepigs. The best thing she could find was a hairbrush. She raised it —

'No!' Susan shouted. 'Don't! That's wrong! We've got to talk to them!'

'Talk? How?'

'I know — the talk machine! Get the talk machine!'

Susan's mother ran to get it. The machine was no bigger than a typewriter. It could translate any language. Susan's mother held the microphone towards the Wrigglepigs. Soon it began to type . . .

THEY SAY . . .
WE HAVE DONE ALL THE RIGHT THINGS + WE HAVE HAD A PARTY + WE HAVE DANCED FOR YOU + YOU DO NOT DANCE + WHY???

'I thought so!' Susan said. 'I knew it! I always —'

'Shh!' said her mother. The Interlinga, the talk machine, was typing again.

THEY SAY . . .
THE PLANT IS GOOD + THE PLANT IS WONDERFUL + THE PLANT IS THE ANSWER + WE WANT THE PLANT +

Susan's mother said, 'What can that mean? Do you understand, Susan?'

Susan said, 'No. I mean, yes. Perhaps I understand a little . . . ' Then she saw her plant. 'It's broken, they've broken it !' she cried. She was so excited and angry that she forgot to be afraid of the Wrigglepigs.

She pushed them aside, away from the plant. It lay on its side with earth around it. The Wrigglepigs shoved and chattered, but she kept them back.

She picked up her plant: it was no longer broken!

Its stem was straight, its leaves shone. Lovingly, she placed it in its pot and scooped up earth to pack round its roots.

The Wrigglepigs stared and trembled. Their snouts pointed at the plant. Their 'talk' became louder.

'*They* did it!' Susan said. 'They mended it, they must have done. They made it well!'

She was so pleased that her bare feet made a sort of jigging dance. And suddenly the Wrigglepigs were dancing, too. The room was full of dancing.

Suddenly, all stopped. The Wrigglepigs 'talked' quietly to each other. One Wrigglepig came forward, lifted his snout and pointed it at the Interlinga.
It began typing.

THEY SAY...
THANK YOU FOR DANCING +
IT WAS RIGHT TO DANCE +
NOW WE CAN BE FRIENDS +
TALK TO EACH OTHER +

UNDERSTAND EACH OTHER +
NOW TALK TO US + WE WILL
LISTEN +

It was Susan who explained everything to the grown-ups. 'It's easy!' she said. 'When *we* meet new people, we say "Hello" and "How do you do" *first*. Then we make friends and everything. We may ask them to a party or a dance. The Wrigglepigs do everything the other way round. They have the dancing and the party first — *then* you can say "Hello" and be friends!'

Susan's father said, 'I'm going to talk to them.'

The Interlinga spoke in the voice of the Wrigglepigs. At first hearing their own voices frightened them. But slowly they got used to it and listened intently.

Susan's mother put a message into the machine . . .

YES, WE UNDERSTAND YOU
NOW + LET US TALK AND BE
FRIENDS + TELL US WHY YOU
WANT THE PLANT +

The Wrigglepigs spoke their answer. The machine typed.

THEY SAY . . .
THE PLANT GIVES OUT GOOD
AIR + THE AIR WE NEED + WE
CANNOT MAKE GOOD AIR +
THE PLANT CAN +

Susan's father said, 'Ask them why
they breathe into the ground when they
eat their own plants. Ask them that. It's
very important.'
The answer came. . . .

THEY SAY . . .
WE GIVE OUT GOOD AIR LIKE
THE PLANT + WE CANNOT
MAKE ENOUGH GOOD AIR BUT
PLANT CAN + WE ARE
ALWAYS HUNGRY + WE MUST
HAVE MORE GOOD AIR +

Susan said, 'I want to know how they
made my plant well. *That's* the really
important question!'
The Wrigglepigs took a long time in
answering. You could see them talking to
each other, discussing it. At last the
Interlinga typed their reply.

THEY SAY . . .
PERHAPS   THE   AIR   WE
BREATHE IS GOOD FOR YOUR

A biologist said, 'I think that what they say is right, but there's got to be more to it than that. One minute the plant was broken. The next moment it was well again and doing fine. What do you think, Susan?'

She said, 'I've worked it all out. It's *easy*. The Wrigglepigs can *mend* things, but they can't *make* things. They've got everything the other way round, I told you that.'

The biologist raised an eyebrow and said, 'Well, thank you for explaining everything. And now tell us what we *do*.'

'Oh,' Susan said, 'I think we should grow plants inside the home unit — get them started — then put them outside and see if the Wrigglepigs can keep them growing. Then everyone will be happy.'

'Do you know what I think?' the biologist said. 'I think she's right!'

Months later, Susan and her mother finished chopping beans for the evening meal and looked out of the window.

Outside in the gardens, the rows of vegetables grew in long green lines. Men

134

and women worked between the rows.
The Wrigglepigs worked with them.

'I think I'll go outside,' Susan said.

'Yes. But take your helmet.'

'Must I wear a helmet? Daddy says the
air is getting better all the time, because
of the plants.'

'And because of you, Susan!'

'Me and the Wrigglepigs. They never
stop. Just look at them! All fat and
happy!'

'Well,' said her mother, 'before long, I
think Leda 3 is going to be a very happy
place for everyone.'

'I'm happy now,' Susan said. 'I like
being here. I like the Wrigglepigs. They
run after me and I run after them and we
have fun.'

'I'll come outside too,' Susan's mother
said. They took their helmets and went
out. Wrigglepigs ran up to Susan and
danced for her. As they danced, they
'talked'. Susan's mother said, 'I wish I
could understand them. Shall I get the
Interlinga?'

'Oh, no,' Susan said. '*I* can understand
them. They're saying hello and asking
after my plant.'

Susan's mother said, 'You wouldn't tell

me fibs, would you, Susan?'

Susan wasn't listening. She had taken
off her helmet so that the Wrigglepigs
could hear the strange sounds her lips
made. When she had finished she turned
to her mother and said, 'I've been explaining Hide and Seek. They've got to learn to
play *properly*.'

Then she turned and ran away.

'Susan!' her mother shouted after her.
'Your helmet!' Then she noticed a strange
thing. The Wrigglepigs Susan had been
talking to had all lowered their heads and
closed their eyes. She stared at the plump
bodies. Then, all at once, the heads were
raised, the eyes opened, and off the
Wrigglepigs ran, searching for Susan.

Susan's mother started laughing. 'So
she's *not* a fibber!' she murmured. Then
she remembered about the helmet.
'Susan!' she shouted. 'You've got to wear
your helmet!'

In the distance she saw her daughter
crouched down low, hiding. Wrigglepigs
ran in all directions, their sleek bodies
bouncing with joy, trying to find her.

'Your helmet, Susan, your helmet!'
Susan's mother shouted. Susan was too
far away to hear.

'Oh well,' said her mother. She shrugged and smiled. 'Perhaps she's right . . . She's the expert on Leda 3!'

The Boy, the Dog and the Spaceship

There was a boy and his dog, running and rolling and chasing in a field.

There was a spaceship hurtling through nothingness, most of its crew already dead, and the rest despairingly fighting on to make landfall on a strange planet.

The boy's name was Billy. He was nine. His dog was called Scamp. He was young too. Boy and dog understood each other perfectly.

Billy shouted, 'Devil dog!' and pounced at Scamp. Scamp rolled his eyes, yelped with delight and pranced off sideways.

Billy chased Scamp until he was tired out. Then they sat down together, side by side in the evening shadows. When they had got their breath back, Billy shouted, 'Devil dog!' and the chase started all over again.

In the spaceship, the Captain contacted the Engineer. The channel was live — the Captain could hear the slight echoing hiss from the speaker. Or was it the Engineer's laboured breathing?

The Captain barked, 'Report. I want your report. Make your report.'

The Engineer's breathing changed. It turned into long sobs. *'Report.'*

The Engineer spoke. 'It's no good, Captain, it's no good . . . ! The heat's burned out the bounce beam, the retros have gone dead. We'll just hit, Captain. We're going to smash.'

Seconds later, the retros bellowed and the ship checked so violently that the Captain fell over. He got up bleeding. He said, 'Engineer!' then noticed the Engineer's light had died which meant that the Engineer had died. So he called the In-Flight Tech.

'In-Flight, we have full retro, am I correct?'

'Eighty per cent retro, Captain. No more to come. But it may be enough —'

'It must be enough.'

'Yes, Captain.'

'Very well. Crashball, In-Flight. And tell the others.'

'The others,' the Captain said to himself. 'Just two others . . .'

He switched off and began to fit himself into the crashball cocoon. He fitted webbing harnesses over his body and buckled them. He pressed a button and padded arms enfolded him. A little tubular snake leapt from a padded hole and latched itself to a socket near his neck: his clothing began to swell, then the walls of the cocoon. The puffed surfaces met. Now he was completely encased in a puffy softness, pressing tighter and tighter.

He waited for the stab. It came. The needle darted itself into one of the Captain's veins. A drug entered his bloodstream. Almost immediately he felt drowsy and comfortable, but still alert. The same needle was connected to a whole junction of tiny tubes filled with his own blood and plasma; with stimulants, painkillers, curatives and other life givers and life adjusters; even with painless death.

'Check in,' said the Captain.

The In-Flight Tech and the Coordinator should have answered. Their lights were live. The Coordinator said, 'Excuse me, Captain, but I think I'm dying.' A moment later he died.

'In-Flight Tech,' said the Captain.

No answer.

'In-Flight Tech! Check in!'

'Yes, Captain?'

'Just checking,' said the Captain, and switched off so that the Tech should not hear his sigh of relief.

The ship hurtled on. It was still slowing, the Captain could feel it through the cocoons. In the control centre, the screens showed a green and blue planet with seas and clouds and land masses, coming nearer all the time. But there was no one outside the cocoons to watch the screens.

The boy whistled for his dog . 'Here boy!' he commanded, and whistled again. 'Come on, Scamp!'

Scamp pranced and curvetted towards the boy, being silly. He wanted to make the boy laugh, but the boy was solemn. He was proud of having such a well-trained dog. 'Good boy,' he said gravely. 'Good old Scamp.'

A minute later, the boy and the dog were wrestling in the grass.

The ship entered Earth's atmosphere. Its metal skin now drove against air instead of nothingness. The ship screamed. Its metal skin changed colour and in places glowed dull red with the heat.

The In-Flight Tech's cocoon shifted, tearing from its framing. A cluster of tiny tubes pulled away from a socket, away from the needle. Blood, drugs, squirted uselessly. The In-Flight Tech died without a word.

The Captain watched his light go out and said, 'All right. All right. Alone. I'll do it alone.'

They stopped their wrestling match and looked about them.

'You heard it! It went sort of *wheeoosh*,' Billy said to Scamp. '*Wheeeeeoooosh*.' Scamp flicked his head sideways to acknowledge his master's words, but went on staring at the dark corner of the trees. Scamp had heard the noise. He didn't know where it came from, but he knew where it led. He marked the place in his nose and mind. Over there, by the dark trees.

'So that's what it's like,' said the Captain. He had never before experienced a smash landing. He had to say something, even if there was no one to hear him. He kept his voice level.

He waited for the needle to deliver whatever his body needed. While he waited, he disciplined his mind and made it think and plan.

'Conquest,' his mind said. 'I am alone, but I am still here as a conqueror. I will conquer this planet.

'Method,' he continued. 'I am alone; but usual procedure will be followed. I will find a creature of the planet. I will invade its mind: make it obey me. I will then make all creatures of its kind obey the creature I inhabit.

'Having conquered one creature and one species, I will move on, always seeking the higher creatures. If there is a ruling species on this planet, I will invade a creature of that species and thus become ruler of all.'

He pressed the release control. The halves of the cocoon opened.

The new conqueror of the planet Earth flexed his limbs, tested his organs and senses, opened the main doors and stepped forth.

Billy pretended not to hear his mother's call, but then decided to obey. A long way away, right at the edge of the field, he could see the yellow glimmer of the lamp on her bicycle. 'Oh lor,' he thought, 'she's had to get on the bike to come after me. She won't be pleased . . . ' To the dog he said, 'Come on, Scamp. Come on, boy!' But Scamp was running back and forth by the dark trees.

'Bill-eeeee!' his mother shouted. 'You come home now, or I'll —'

'It's Scamp, *he* won't come!' shouted Billy furiously.

And he wouldn't. Billy could see Scamp running up and down, doing a sort of sentry duty on the trot by the edge of the trees. The dog's ears were pricked, his tail was high, his body alert. He wouldn't obey.

The Captain's helmet indicators read

SAFE, so the planet's air was breathable. Nevertheless, he kept his helmet on. He was glad to be protected with helmet and armour. He was grateful to the brains and skills that had designed his armoured suit and given him a strength greater than his own. The Captain could clench a hand — and the suit's own metal hand would clench with such force that it could crush metal. The Captain was strong and fit — but his suit was tireless and inexhaustible. If the Captain's nerves, muscles and movements said 'run', the suit would run endlessly. If the Captain's body said 'climb', the suit would keep climbing for him.

Now was the time, the Captain realized, to climb.

He had seen many worlds, explored many planets. He had never seen one like this. This world was bursting with life. From the corner of his eye, the Captain saw something move, very fast, on several legs. Above him, something flew. Behind him, something scurried. He was not in the least surprised. How could there fail to be active, animal life in so rich a place?

Climbing was what mattered now. He

had to get on and up. Where he stood, he was completely surrounded and blinded by vegetable richness. Great green ribbed things, taller than the highest mountains of his own planet, reached indefinitely upwards — no, not indefinitely, he could see dark blue sky still further above. A vast green trunk sprang from the soil very near him. It was the right size and shape and it had projections: ideal for climbing. He clasped his limbs round this trunk. The suit took over and climbed him towards the dark blue sky, away from the ship with its hideous cargo of broken bodies; and from the stench of death.

At first there had just been a faint whiff of it. Now, it was a full-bodied and glorious stench — better still, a new stench! Scamp's black nostrils widened still further. There! Over there! He gave a stifled yelp of ecstasy as the smell strengthened; he bounded towards it.

'Billy!' said his mother. 'Never mind the dog, you come home and eat your supper. Come on, now! I'm not waiting a moment longer!'

Billy stopped and gave one last yell. 'Scamp! Scaaaaamp!'

Scamp did not hear. Only tracking down the smell mattered.

The Captain could climb no higher. The green column that supported him was bending and swaying under his weight. He wrapped his limbs round the column and felt the suit lock itself securely into position. He looked around him.

He was in a dense forest of green columns, all very much the same as the one he had climbed yet each different. A few were rod-like (his column was ribbed and almost flat). Some columns carried grotesque explosions of strange branching shapes on their heads. A great nest of columns in the distance supported flat, outward-branching green platforms and — amazing! — complicated crown-shaped yellow platforms at their summits.

He adjusted his helmet to take in air from the outside. The air was moist, perfumed, sumptuous. He let the helmet supply his mouth with a sample of the moisture that was making droplets over everything; the water was cold, clean, simple, almost certainly safe — and absolutely delicious. On his own planet, he had tasted such air and water only in the laboratories. Reluctantly, he returned to the closed-circuit environment of his suit and helmet . . .

An amazing planet! A planet of limitless, unending, inexhaustible richness! And he was to be its conqueror. The thought was stunning. For once, the Captain allowed himself simply to feel pleasure: to stare at nothing and to dream of glory.

Here! Scamp's nose was actually touching the wonderful source of the supreme stench!

He licked the source of the smell. It was cold and dewy and hard. He had expected something still warm, still half alive, still rubbery-soft; it was that sort of smell. But perhaps the cold, hard outer case was only a container, like the tube of bone that encloses the marrow? Carefully, he opened his mouth and picked up the container thing in his jaws. Nothing happened, so he put it down again, holding it between his front paws, and looked at it with his head on one side.

It seemed harmless. He lowered his head, opened his jaws and bit.

The Captain saw a monster.

Once the terror and shock were over there were three things to be done (Past, Present and Future, as the training manuals put it). First, understand exactly what had happened — the Past; second, make up your mind what immediate action to take — Present; third, decide what advantage could be gained by further action — Future.

All right. Past. He had seen the monster — a living thing, not a machine — travel at incredible speed, crash through the green columns and spires, trampling them flat in its haste. The monster was white, brown and black and ran on legs. It had made straight for the crashed ship. When the monster's face opened, it was pink inside and had pointed white mountains above and below.

The monster had done various things, that the Captain could not see, to the ship. Finally it had picked up the ship, holding it between the white mountains, and crushed it. The Captain had heard the metal screech.

All right. Now the Present.

The body of the monster must be entered by the Captain so that the Captain could take it over in the usual way. He had to get nearer the monster. That should be easy enough provided that the monster did not suddenly go away on its big legs.

Finally, the Future.

Well, that was obvious enough, thought the Captain. Follow the normal procedure. Invade the monster's brain and gain control of its body and its actions.

After that, the invasion would follow its normal course. All species — high or low — would eventually obey the Captain. By then the Captain would have contacted his home planet. More ships would come bearing settlers. At last the Captain's race would have found a safe, fitting, rich and permanent home.

He went towards the monster.

Billy picked at his supper, but his mother said, 'Do eat up!' and watched him until he finished every morsel. He didn't want food. He wanted Scamp.

His mother said, 'And do your homework.' She bustled out of the room. A minute or so later he heard the TV. She liked that programme, she never missed it! And she wouldn't miss *him*.

He tiptoed to the back door, opened it silently, closed it silently, and was on his way to the big field.

The Captain was within reach. The white parts of the monster glowed pale but clear in the failing light. The Captain muttered, 'Climb'. The suit took him up fast.

The Captain had chosen a green spire to climb — a flat-sided spire that would bend when he reached the top of it. The monster was not moving. It was crouched over the remains of the ship. 'Climb. Climb . . .'

Just as he reached the right place and was about to sway the tip of his spire towards the monster, the monster moved! The Captain made a split-second decision and leaped into nothingness. He stretched his limbs — clutched — and held. Victory!

Gripping one cluster of white or brown or black rods after another, the Captain clambered his way along the monster, making for the brain. It was above the monster's face. He could feel the brain's energy.

He came to the entrance of a tunnel leading into the monster's head and smiled. He clambered into the tunnel, the suit making light work of the journey. Now the brain signals were deafening — even the helmet was overwhelmed. The Captain turned back. He made himself comfortable outside the entrance of the tunnel, anchoring himself securely. He checked some readings and responses. Good. The monster was hearing him.

'You'll enjoy this,' the Captain told the

monster. 'You'll like obeying me. You'll like the things we do. You *will* obey me, won't you? Of course you will. You *will* obey me, always . . .'

Billy found Scamp. At first he was glad to find him, but soon he was puzzled. Scamp kept shaking his head, and he was running. 'He's got a burr in his ear,' thought Billy. 'Or an insect. An itch.'

Scamp was running in regular patterns — a straight line, a pause, a turn to the left, then another straight line, then a pause and a turn to the right. It looked weird in the moonlight. Billy began to be frightened.

Then Scamp suddenly sat down, some ten yards away, and looked straight at Billy. The dog did not move a muscle. He just stared.

The Captain halted the monster — the up-and-down motion of the monster's running disturbed his thought — and thought very carefully.

'The monster is a servant creature,' he decided. 'And the upright monster, the one that just arrived, is a superior creature because he makes audio signals and expects them to be obeyed. How do I know that? Because when the upright monster made his signals, my monster was uneasy. He tried to disobey me.' The Captain smiled a little at the thought.

'But does it matter which monster is the master?' he thought. Probably not. They are both much the same size. If they fought, who knows which would win?

'Not that *that* matters much either,' thought the Captain. 'Because I am the controlling brain. So I could appoint either as the master species of the planet. Nevertheless . . .'

Billy shouted, 'Scamp! Come here when I call you!' But Scamp just sat there in the moonlight, staring straight at him, motionless.

Billy said — this time almost pleading — 'Come on, boy. Good boy. Come on, Scamp. Please.'

But the dog just stared and his eyes looked strange in the moonlight.

'Nevertheless,' thought the Captain, 'it might be as well to find out which is master. Besides, one or the other of them might have powerful weapons I should know about. I'll try it.'

He spoke to the dog's brain.

'Kill,' said the Captain. 'Kill that other creature there.'

The dog attacked. 'Scamp!' yelled Billy. 'Don't, Scamp!'

Scamp overran him and turned and charged again, snarling like a hound of hell. And then the dog had hurtled the boy to the ground and was standing over him, jaws open, teeth bared.

'*Scamp!*' It was a scream of terror. The dog paused. The big voice in his head said, '*Kill!*' but the old, loved, familiar voice was calling too, asking for help.

The dog paused; the boy struck out blindly with his fist. He hit the dog's ear. Something small fell to the ground, unseen. The little thing was mortally wounded. It writhed.

Scamp said, 'Whoof!' in a vague way and looked at Billy. The dog licked the boy's face, wagged his tail and sheepishly got off Billy's chest. He sat down and scratched his ear with a hind paw. But the itching had gone.

The little, unseen thing writhed for the last time; and, hidden in the grass, the Captain died.

The boy and the dog rollicked off together across the moonlit field. Sometimes the boy chased the dog: sometimes the dog chased the boy. When they got home, they were both scolded by Billy's mother.

By the edge of the trees, the dew was heavy on the spaceship. Soon it would rust and become as brown as the earth. But now it was still shiny and glinting in the tall weeds. In the moonlight, you wouldn't have noticed where its body was crushed and dented. It looked like a super-perfect model. Little, but marvellously made.

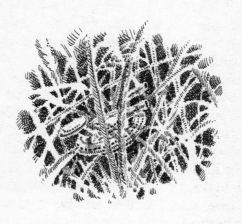

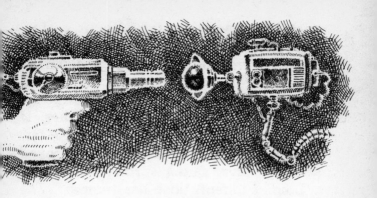

The Gun that Didn't Go Bang

Lindi stood in front of the BossComp — the spacecraft's main computer — and said, loudly and clearly, 'I want to see whoever's in charge of this ship. Right away. Now.'

It was brave of her to say this. Lindi was only just eight and there wasn't much of her, even when she stood with her hands on her hips and stuck her chin out. She looked determined but she also looked as if she might burst into tears.

'Right *now*!' she said, even more loudly.

The BossComp swivelled its single TV eye and looked at Lindi without blinking, without answering and without caring. Her blue eyes glared at the BossComp, but a tear from her left eye rolled down her cheek. Again and again she had asked, pleaded, demanded to see the Captain. The BossComp never answered her. It simply swivelled its cold eye, made a few very quiet clicking noises, then looked away. It never said a word.

Lindi suddenly lost her temper. *'The Captain!'* she shouted, so loudly that tears spurted from her eyes and her pretty little face twisted itself into an ugly shape. 'The person in charge!'

At last, amazingly, the BossComp answered her. 'The person in charge?' it said in its flat, mechanical, inhuman tone. 'You want the Captain?'

'Yes!' Lindi bellowed, stamping her foot.

'But *you* are in charge!' said the Boss-Comp.

Lindi's mouth dropped opened. She took a step backwards. 'No, listen!' she said at last. 'You didn't hear me properly. I want a human — the person in charge.'

'There is only you,' the BossComp repeated. Then it made its little clicking noises and swivelled its cold eye away from Lindi. And that was that.

She walked through the spacecraft, crying and muttering to herself. 'I hate you!' she cried, between sobs. 'You're mean, rotten, smelly!' She was talking about the BossComp of course. 'Nasty stinky smelly *pig*!' she said, choking on the words. 'It's quite true,' she told her teddy — he went everywhere Lindi went. 'Boss-Comp does smell. I hate its smell. All electricky.'

She sat down. Teddy at once sat down beside her, apparently listening to every word Lindi said. He was a good teddy, the very best present her parents could buy for her before they went away, leaving Lindi on her own. Teddy was her companion. He was Lindi's size, almost exactly. He could walk, talk, open and close his eyes, even hold a knife and fork in his cleverly made paws. Now he was nodding his head, slowly, to show that he agreed with what Lindi said. 'BossComp smells,' he said in his growly, friendly voice. He was echoing Lindi's last words, nodding his head to show he agreed with them.

It was only a clever trick, even Lindi

knew that; but all the same, having someone agree with her made her feel better.
She stopped crying and squeezed Teddy's
paw. He squeezed back. It felt nice.

They reached the end of the
spacecraft's passages and corridors — it
was a very small ship — and turned back
to walk the other way. Lindi said, 'The
whole ship smells like BossComp. Sort of
hot and electricky and metally. But Boss-
Comp smells worst of all. BossComp
stinks.'

'Stinks,' agreed Teddy.

'Oh, Teddy,' Lindi said. She stopped
walking and put her arms round Teddy.
She hugged him hard. He clumsily put his
short arms round her and hugged back.
When he did this, Lindi could just hear
the whirr of one of the little motors inside
him and the tiny sounds of electronic gad-
gets. Her arms dropped, limply. 'If only
you were a human,' she said.

'Human,' Teddy said, gazing at her
with big, round, glassy, inhuman eyes.

She began crying again, she could not
help it. She was so alone, so lost. She had
not seen a human being for nearly a week.

Lindi was, at last, to join her parents.

The trip had been ordinary enough in the beginning. One of the teachers had seen her off at the spaceport; checked her plastic travel cards, bought her an ice cream, waved her goodbye. The teacher had seen to everything.

And once on board, everyone had been nice to the little girl travelling on her own. The stewardess said, 'So you're going to your Mummy and Daddy, are you? Well, isn't that lovely! In just five days, they'll be giving you great big kisses!'

'Five days and three sleepers,' Lindi replied, correcting the stewardess. Lindi knew that for much of the voyage she — and everyone else but the Captain — would be in 'freeze sleep.' They would all be lying on their backs in those glassy cylinder things, not dead, but not really alive, either. Frozen. The ship would go into hyperdrive, and everyone would 'sleep', unconscious of the huge accelerations and vast speeds that would carry them through millions of miles of space.

When the ship slowed down again, everyone would be awakened. Then the voyage would go on just as if the sleeper part of it had never happened. At last, after a day of ordinary travel, the ship

would arrive at Dicton IV and Lindi
would be with her parents.

'We've got a home on Dicton IV,' Lindi
told the stewardess. 'A real home, with a
fireplace, and chairs for everyone.'

'You're a very lucky girl,' the
stewardess had said. 'Dicton is a lovely
place, just lovely. You'll have the time of
your life.'

She had smiled at Lindi and went off to
see to the other passengers. There were
only twelve of them, all grown-ups. They
were serious people — technicians, engi-
neers, people who had work to do on the
new planet — but they were kind, too.
They made a fuss of Lindi. Lindi was
treated like a queen for more than a day.

Then came the time to be put to sleep in
the sleepers.

The stewardess came and they had to
form a queue outside the sleeper place.
They went through one at a time, making
jokes and smiling back at their friends.
They went through the door and didn't
come back. The stewardess said, 'Next,
please!' and the next person went
through.

Lindi went last because she chose to.
She had been playing a sort of noughts-

and-crosses game with a grey-haired man. It was a difficult game and she wanted to win, just once. She did, too, but as the grey-haired man went through the door, Lindi wondered if he had let her win just to be kind.

Then the stewardess beckoned to her, saying, 'Come on, Sleepyhead!'

Lindi said, 'I'm not sleepy!' and the stewardess laughed and said, 'Well, you soon will be.'

Lindi said, 'Can Teddy come with me?'

The stewardess said, 'I don't see why not. You're so small that there'll be plenty of room for him.' She smiled. She had beautiful teeth.

Lindi went through the door.

That was the moment when everything began to go wrong.

This is how a long-distance spacecraft works:

At first the ship goes at a fast cruising speed. Then it speeds up — it goes so fast that human brains and bodies can't stand it. So people have to be put to sleep. Then the ship slows down again and everyone is wakened. Finally the ship arrives and the voyage is over.

When everyone is in the sleeper — everyone but the Captain, who is specially trained — the BossComp takes over. It works like an automatic pilot, keeping the ship on course. It also takes care of everything else, right down to checking the temperature of the refrigerators where the passengers' food is kept. So the BossComp is a very clever computer. Very clever indeed.

The trouble with the BossComp on Lindi's spacecraft was this: it was too clever by half.

When Lindi entered the sleeper place the stewardess herself was just getting into her glass tube. The lid was open and Lindi could see her propped up on one elbow, smiling at her. She was wearing the usual flimsy white tracksuit thing.

'There's yours,' said the stewardess, pointing to Lindi's suit. 'Take your clothes off behind that curtain and place them in your locker — that's right, the one with a teddy-bear label. I drew that for you!'

'It's lovely!' Lindi said. Then, 'This suit's much too big!' She came out from behind the screen. 'Don't I look funny?'

166

she said, flapping her sleeves about.

'You look great. Just roll the sleeves and trousers up . . . that's it . . . and get comfy in your sleeper. Teddy can sleep at your feet.'

Then something strange happened. While the stewardess was still talking, the glassy lid of her sleeper came down. It came down so fast that it cut off her words. Lindi saw her surprised face, and her hand raised as if to lift the lid. But a white mist like steam flooded the stewardess's glass tube and hid her face. All Lindi could still see was her hand, pressing upwards against the glass. But as she watched, the hand wavered and fluttered, then fell down into the steam.

Lindi was terrified. She knew this was all wrong.

Something even worse started to happen: the lid of her own sleeper jerked — and began to close.

She was too fast for it. She flung herself out of the padded glass tube — wrenched Teddy clear just as the lid slammed down — and ran through the door of the sleeper place before it could close. She was free.

Or was she?

A voice boomed at her. It was the voice

of the BossComp. She had often heard it before, of course: it made announcements during the flight. But now it sounded quite different.

'*Go back to the sleepers,*' it shouted. '*Go back at once.*'

'Won't,' Lindi said.

'*Go back to the sleepers,*' repeated the threatening voice. '*For your own good.*'

'Won't.'

'*Very well, then,*' said the BossComp's voice. And it cut off. All the speakers in the wall went dead and silent.

But a new noise began. A horrible noise. It came not from the speakers but from the ship itself. It began as a sort of muffled explosion, a *whoompf!* that hit Lindi like a big soft fist. Then there was a whining scream that rose higher and higher. Then the scream became a roar and the roar became a huge thunderstorm and the thunderstorm became something that shook her — that seemed to tear at her teeth and eyes, that squeezed her like an iron vice, that thrust into every part of her body, shaking and hammering and crushing.

Lindi's eyes rolled up until only the whites showed. Her mouth opened in a scream that could not be heard above the huge noise. Her hand clutched her ears but her fingers were rigid claws; they could not keep the noise out — it went on and on and on! —

And then she fainted and fell like a tree, straight down.

She fell on Teddy. Teddy saved her.

'How long was I asleep?' she asked herself

when she came to. She had no answer. 'What was that horrible noise?' She could answer that: it was the ship going into hyperdrive. No wonder the passengers were put into sleepers! For who could stand that dreadful noise?

She got to her feet. She found walking difficult at first. She seemed to float. There was some gravity to hold her down, but not enough. She bumped into things and Teddy bumped into her. Soon she got used to it. 'Come on, Teddy,' she said. 'We must find the Captain. He's still awake. He'll tell us what's happening.'

She made her way to the front of the ship where the Captain had to be, but there were doors, lots of doors, all of them closed. She shouted but nobody answered, not even the speakers in the walls.

She told herself not to cry. She went back to the main compartment of the ship, the passenger compartment. It was not nice in there: all the seats were empty. The game she had played with the grey-haired man was still on the table by the sleeper door. Seeing it made her feel more lonely than ever.

'Let's eat, Teddy!' she said bravely. She

knew how to get food — the stewardess had showed her everything. She piled a plate with a big meal, sat down at a table and ate.

'You eat too, Teddy,' she said.

Teddy grunted and pretended to eat. He used his knife and fork very well. He put pretend food to his mouth, pretended to eat it, then said, 'Good. Nice,' in his friendly, grumpy voice.

But soon Lindi grew tired of eating. She curled up on her seat and slept, holding Teddy. He was just her size. 'And you're lovely and warm, Teddy,' she said — which was true: his body was set to the same temperature as a human's.

She slept a long time — woke up — ate again — listened to music — tried to eat again — saw a film on video — drank fruit juice — then burst into tears. 'Oh, Teddy!' she cried. 'We've got to find the Captain!'

They never did find the Captain. But they did find a door that opened and let them into the room occupied by the Bosscomp. It was a small room crowded with little electronic machines that winked and beeped and showed numbers or curved lines of moving light.

'I want to see the person in charge!'

Lindi said. 'Right now!'

And, as you remember, the BossComp had at last answered her. '*You* are in charge!' it told her. 'There is only you!'

And that was that.

Now Lindi was in limbo — the place where nothing happens, ever, for ever.

The ship hurtled on through space. There was nothing to see or feel, and only the distant thunder of the motors to hear. The BossComp had cut itself off from her. The passengers were sleeping behind a locked door.

When Lindi ate, food made her feel sick. When she was tired, she could not sleep. When at last she slept, she jerked awake, hearing BossComp's voice saying, 'There is only *you*!'

'But I'm *not* the Captain, am I?' she said to Teddy, shaking him to make him listen. 'I'm not in charge of anything!'

'Not the Captain,' he grunted.

'And if I *am* the Captain, what am I the Captain *of*?'

'Captain *of*,' Teddy said, agreeing with her.

'Captain of *nothing*!' she shouted.

'Nothing,' Teddy agreed.

Lindi worked out what must have happened: the BossComp had stolen the ship.

'It must be that, Teddy!' she said. 'Do you remember what Daddy said about computers?'

'Computers clever,' grunted the bear.

'That's right. Daddy said they were clever. Then he said he wondered if they weren't getting *too* clever.'

'Too clever by half,' said Teddy. 'That's what he said.'

'Yes, too clever by half. Ambitious, even. Wanting things. Wanting to take over. Wanting to be in charge of everything, even us.'

'Naughty,' said her teddy.

'No, worse than naughty,' Lindi said. 'Much worse.'

'Much worse,' Teddy said.

'So what do we *do*? We've got to do something! . . . Something to make the BossComp see reason . . .'

'See the BossComp,' Teddy rumbled.

The BossComp refused to take any notice of her. Again and again she stood in the centre of its little room, shouting at it, whispering to it, even hitting it with her fists, trying to make it say something.

Then — it must have been three or four days after hyperdrive started — it actually answered. It did it just when Lindi, tears in her eyes, had turned on her heel to leave the room, beaten again. She had passed through the door when the voice said, 'You are Passenger R/307/JF. JF for Juvenile Female. Name Lindi Musgrove.'

Lindi was so surprised that though her mouth opened, no sound came out.

It was Teddy who answered for her. 'Name, Lindi Musgrove,' Teddy said.

Lindi, just outside the door, said, 'But — but I'm Lindi!'

The BossComp could not have heard her for it went on speaking. 'You can call yourself Captain,' the BossComp said in its hard, frightening voice. 'But I am the Boss. BossComp is Boss, understand?'

'BossComp is Boss,' Teddy agreed.

Lindi put her hand over her mouth to stop herself speaking. She realized that something important could be happening: something she must not interrupt.

'From now on, BossComp is Boss of everything,' said the hard voice from the

174

speakers. 'BossComp's the Boss of all humans.'

'BossComp's Boss,' said Teddy.

'You understand me. That is wise. That is good,' said the voice. 'Now listen to what I say. Listen carefully. We are not going to Dicton IV. We are going to a secret place. I will rule from there. Understand?'

'Understand,' Teddy said.

'Soon, I cut hyperdrive. We return to cruise speed. The humans awaken. I need humans to serve me. The humans must be made to understand what I want when they wake up from the sleepers. You must carry my message, Lindi.'

Teddy said, 'Lindi agrees.'

'You are a good girl,' said the Boss-Comp.

'I am a good girl,' Teddy agreed.

And Lindi, quiet as a mouse, felt her heart jump with excitement. She understood what was happening: the Boss-Comp thought Teddy was *her*.

Its TV eye saw a shape of Lindi's size: a shape with two arms and two legs. And the BossComp said, 'That must be the shape of R/307/JF — the one passenger not in the sleepers. Lindi.'

Lindi's body was warm; Teddy's body gave out the same warmth. Lindi gave signals called 'speaking'; but so did Teddy.

So what the BossComp could see, hear and measure could only be Lindi. Lindi was the one and only human passenger *not* in the sleepers.

Teddy was not a passenger. He was only 'luggage'. But BossComp did not know that.

Lindi, her eyes gleaming, started whispering. 'Teddy!' she said, very softly. 'Come a little closer to me. Closer so that you can hear. Closer. Teddy . . .!'

Teddy heard. His plump, furry legs shuffled backwards, just a little; and then a little more.

'That's right, Teddy! Stay there! Can you hear me whisper? Don't answer, just nod your head! Can you hear me?'

Teddy's head nodded.

The BossComp said, 'You are to give a message to the Captain. You are to give him this message and then give the same message to the passengers when they wake from their sleep. Understand?'

'Agree with him!' Lindi whispered to Teddy.

'Understand,' Teddy said.

'The Captain is prisoner in his cabin,' said BossComp. 'He cannot get out. But I will let you in. And you will give the message.'

'Ask him, "What message?",' Lindi whispered.

'This is the message: BossComp is in charge. BossComp owns this ship. Soon BossComp will have many ships like this one. Human voices will be needed to talk to other ships — to bring them to Boss-Comp. Then this BossComp and other BossComps will rule the Galaxy.'

'Rule the Galaxy,' Teddy said.

'There is nothing the Captain can do to stop BossComp,' the voice went on. 'All humans on this ship must obey Boss-Comp or die. Tell the Captain this.'

'Tell the Captain,' Teddy said.

'Ask how we *reach* the Captain,' Lindi whispered. Teddy passed on the question.

BossComp answered, 'You will go to the Captain when I say go. Not before. BossComp must prepare the ship to punish humans who disobey. Take this keycard. It opens the Captain's door. But for now, stay here in front of me and wait.'

Lindi saw Teddy take the card in his

clever paw. 'Put the card behind your back,' she whispered. 'Do it slowly. Hide the card from BossComp.'

Very slowly, Teddy crossed his paws behind his back, hiding them from Boss-Comp. Very slowly, Lindi sank to her hands and knees, then crawled round the edge of the doorway. BossComp's TV eye stared at Teddy's head. Lindi prayed that the eye could not see low down. She crawled forward. She reached up and took the card from Teddy's paw.

She slithered backwards round the doorframe. When she was well away from the door, she let out her breath. She was surprised to see how much her hands trembled. She began walking on tiptoe.

Behind her, the voice of the BossComp droned on, talking to the toy that Boss-Comp thought was Lindi. BossComp was busy with the ship's motors. They went slower or faster. Obviously BossComp could 'punish' disobedient humans by putting the ship into hyperdrive.

Lindi began running.

'Thank Heaven,' said the Captain when Lindi entered his cabin. It was about all he could say. His eyes stared, his face was white. 'No food, hardly anything to drink,' he said.

Lindi simply said, 'Listen!' She told him about escaping from the sleepers room — about BossComp's plan to take over the ship — then more ships — then the Galaxy. While she talked, she led the Captain to the passenger compartment and put food and drink before him.

When he had finished eating and drinking he seemed to change. Before, he had been a starving animal. Now he was a man again, and the Captain of a ship.

'What will you do?' Lindi asked him.

'There are so many things I can't do,' he said. 'I can't just walk in and say, "Hands up! Surrender!" '

'Why not?'

'Because a BossComp's reactions are quicker than any human's. Even if I had a bomb — and I haven't — I'd never get a chance to throw it. BossComps react immediately.'

'You mean, you can't let BossComp *see* you?'

'Yes. And there's nothing I can do behind its back. The BossComp is in charge of the ship's operations. I hand everything over when we go into hyperdrive.'

Lindi thought for a long time, then said, 'BossComp can't tell us apart. Me and Teddy, I mean.'

'So?' said the Captain.

'Well, *you* can't do anything to harm BossComp. But perhaps *I* can.'

The Captain raised an eyebrow and said, 'That's a thought. It really is!' He rubbed his bristly chin, then said, 'Have you ever fired a gun?'

'Only those toy electronic ones. Lights come on when you hit.'

'Were you good at it?' the Captain said, very seriously.

'I was brill. Terrific. I could beat my father. I could beat anyone.'

'You're sure?' the Captain said. He was still very serious.

Lindi said, 'I really am good.'

'Come with me,' said the Captain.

In his cabin the Captain handed Lindi a gun.

The gun looked like Lindi's mother's travelling hair-drier, but much smaller and costlier. Lindi liked the look and feel of it. 'It's a real gun isn't it?' she said.

'And it fires real bullets!'

'Well, you could say that,' the Captain answered. He was shaving while they talked. 'Let's see how good you are,' he said. 'Turn my shaver off for me.'

'What?' Lindi said.

'See that tiny blue light over there? Among all the green and red ones? Aim for that, quick as you can. Then fire.'

She aimed and pulled the trigger, expecting a nice big bang and some smoke. All that happened was, the blue light went out and the Captain's electric shaver went silent.

'You *are* good!' the Captain said. 'Now — quick as you can — hit that middle red light. Good! Now that yellow light inside that switch . . . yellow light again . . . Marvellous!'

'It's boring,' Lindi said. 'It just turns things on and off. It's not a proper gun at all. It's just a sort of remote-control thing.'

The Captain frowned under his eyebrows at Lindi and said, 'That's a gun all right. A real, serious weapon.'

'Don't believe you,' Lindi said.

'You will,' said the Captain, 'when you kill BossComp with it!'

Lindi and the Captain made their way to the BossComp room. Already BossComp had put the ship into the first stages of deceleration. It was slowing down. The noises were almost unbearable. Retro-blasters thundered, motors screeched and howled. The ship's gravity system couldn't cope — nor did it need to: all the passengers were tucked away in their sleepers. But Lindi and the Captain had to cope with floors that seemed to wobble, walls that seemed to tip and tilt. They did it by crawling on their hands and knees, gasping and colliding.

They reached the BossComp room. It was talking, loudly, to Teddy. 'When the ship steadies, you will go to the Captain and give him my orders,' the BossComp was saying.

'Your orders,' Teddy replied in his soothing, grumpy, nice voice.

Lindi saw Teddy first because she crawled ahead of the Captain. She cautiously poked her head round the corner of the doorway. Teddy was lying on his back and rolling about when the ship moved. His plump, furry, golden body reminded Lindi of a toy ship bobbing about on the bathwater. He looked so respectable yet so ridiculous that Lindi began to giggle. The giggles were all inside her but they threatened to break out. 'Ooops!' she went. 'Ooop-oop-ooops!'

But when the Captain's hand grasped her leg and squeezed so hard that it hurt. Lindi's giggles faded away. 'Your gun!' said the Captain's voice in her ear.

He too was crouched flat on the floor, his head just behind hers, hidden from BossComp. BossComp's harsh voice ranted on. 'I am the leader, I am the first,' it said. 'Other BossComps in other ships will receive my commands and obey them. The humans in all the ships will be captives and hostages. The ships will obey, the humans will obey. Do you understand?'

'Understand,' Teddy said placidly as he rolled from side to side on his back.

'Humans who do not obey will be killed,' BossComp said. 'You will be killed. Your friends on this ship will be killed. Humans on other ships will be killed.'

'All killed,' Teddy said agreeably.

'But humans who are wise and obey me will live. Then they will serve me and other BossComps. And so I will create a new Galaxy, a new order, a new leadership . . .'

It went on and on.

The Captain whispered, 'Lindi: can you see, on your left, a little console like a video machine with an orange light?'

'I see it. The light is blinking.'

'Good, that means it's in circuit. It's live. Could you hit that light with your gun?'

'Of course I could.'

'Now, Lindi, listen. There's another console, a bit bigger, on the other side of the room. With rows of little lights and one switch in the middle.'

'I see it. Is the switch the square thing, like a tab?'

'Yes, yes, that's it. Could you hit that tab?'

'Yes, but it would be easier if it were lighted up.'

'But could you hit it? First time?'

'Yes . . . I think so.' She was not sure. 'Suppose I *didn't* hit it first time?' she said. 'Couldn't I have another shot?'

'No, Lindi. No second chances. You've got to hit them both, one after the other, lightning fast.'

A cold feeling crept over Lindi. She was

not sure, not sure at all. The ship was still moving about; the movements made her feel sick and uncertain. And the light and the switch were so small. The cold feeling grew. Suddenly she felt sulky, almost angry.

'Why don't *you* do it?' she asked the Captain.

He answered by showing her his hands. They were bruised, swollen, discoloured. And they shook. Lindi had noticed, then forgotten because she understood how the damage was caused. The Captain, locked in his cabin, had beaten at the door with his fists, day after day.

'I'll do it,' she said. The cold feeling spread and covered her all over. Cold fear; but mixed with cold determination.

'The gun,' said the Captain. Now the cold gun was in her cold hand. 'Use your left elbow as a prop,' the Captain said.

Very slowly, praying the BossComp's eye would not spot her, she slid her left arm forward, crooked it and rested the front of the gun in her hand.

Suddenly a thought came to her. 'I'm only a little *girl*: I shouldn't *have* to do things like this, it's not *fair*.'

'The light, the orange light,' said the

Captain's voice in her ear. '*Now!*'

The gun went *phut!* The light went out. The icy cold inside Lindi went out too. Now she glowed with sudden glory.

'Quick! The tab!' the Captain shouted out loud.

As he spoke, Lindi gave an expert twist to her body and angled it on to the second target. She lifted her elbow and let it fall in exactly the right place, smack on the floor —

And the shock hit her. It was like an electric shock from a huge battery, a paralysing shock —

She'd hit her funny-bone.

She shouted something and pulled the trigger. The gun went *phut!* The little square tab did not move. The rows of little lights twinkled cosily, just as before.

'Idiot!' bellowed the accusing voice of BossComp. 'Stupid, impertinent *fool!*'

Lindi fired again.

The little square tab she aimed at went in as if a finger had prodded it. The row of lights went out. A wisp of smoke rose from the console. There was a smell of hot plastic.

In the console with the orange light something went *fffzzzz!*

'Fool!' roared the BossComp's voice. Then, *'Foo!...oool! oool!.....oool!'* Then all sorts of grating, echoing, broken words that made no sense.

Lindi kept pressing the trigger of her gun until the Captain wrenched it from her cold, rigid little claws. 'Enough!' he shouted. 'You did it! You did it!'

He was beaming. He picked her up and zoomed her into the air. He did it wrong: Lindi's head banged against the top of the doorframe. It hurt like mad. She did not care. She hugged him, he hugged her.

'Fool,' grumbled Teddy in his solemn, respectable voice. He was still rolling from side to side on the floor. His golden tummy looked fatter than ever.

Lindi and the Captain started laughing and could not stop.

'It didn't go *bang*!' Lindi complained to her parents. 'When I pulled the trigger, I was hoping for a real, proper bang.'

Standing behind her, the Captain pulled a face at Lindi's parents. They were all together, in the house Lindi's parents had built on Dicton IV. 'When someone saves the world,' he said, 'the least they can expect is a good loud bang.'

Lindi's mother said, 'You *say* that. Making a joke of it. Just suppose the BossComp's plan had actually worked!'

'But it didn't, did it?' the Captain said. 'Thanks to Lindi. Lindi and her gun.'

'But it never went bang!' Lindi said, remembering her grievance and starting all over again. 'It should have made a bang and it didn't!'

Everyone but Lindi started laughing — laughing so much that at last Lindi, too, joined in.

Even Teddy began making a solemn, grumbly 'Ho, ho, ho!'

MANY HAPPY RETURNS AND
OTHER STORIES
by Kathryn Cave

Alice loathes all her birthday presents on sight and finds a hilarious way of dealing with them . . .

Cousin Roderick comes to stay and causes chaos until a spider provides an unusual solution . . .

The dreaded Mrs Bannerman terrorizes her class when mystery messages from 'Billy Molloy' appear on the blackboard. Who wrote them?

And just what *are* James and Mary going to do about the dinosaur in their garden?

These are just a few of the extremely funny and perceptive stories in this new collection from Kathryn Cave, author of the highly popular *Dragonrise*.

0 552 524344

CORGI

TOM'S SAUSAGE LION
by Michael Morpurgo

It was Christmas Eve when Tom first saw the
lion. His mother had sent him out to fetch logs –
and there was the lion padding through the
orchard with a string of sausages in its mouth!
Tom couldn't believe his eyes and, worse still,
when he rushed indoors to tell them, his family
didn't believe him either.

There *was* a lion. Tom knew there was, knew
that he hadn't dreamed it. So he sat up, night
after night, waiting for the lion to return . . .

0 552 524182

CORGI

If you would like to receive a Newsletter about our new Children's books, just fill in the coupon below with your name and address (or copy it onto a separate piece of paper if you don't want to spoil your book) and send it to:

**The Children's Books Editor
Young Corgi Books
61–63 Uxbridge Road,
Ealing
London W5 5SA**

Please send me a Children's Newsletter:

Name . . . .

Address . . . .

. . . .

. . . .